MONSTER DINOSAUR

MONSTER DINOSAUR

Daniel Cohen

J.B. Lippincott New York

Illustration credits: American Museum of Natural History, 23, 72–73; *Animals: 1419 Copyright-Free Illustrations of Mammals, Birds, Fish, Insects, etc.*, selected by Jim Harter (New York: Dover Publications, 1979), 12, 20, 44, 91; Carnegie Museum of Natural History, 39; *The Day of the Dinosaur*, by L. Sprague de Camp and Catherine Crook de Camp (New York: Doubleday, 1968), 18, 131; *The Dinosaur Coloring Book*, by Anthony Rao (New York: Dover Publications, 1980), 51, 54, 65, 89; *A Journey to the Earth's Interior, or Have the Poles Really Been Discovered?* by Marshall B. Gardner (Aurora, Illinois: Eugene Smith Company, 1920), 134; Loch Ness Phenomenon Investigation Bureau, 112; *Movie Star News*, 149; *Mythical Beasts Coloring Book*, by Fridolf Johnson (New York: Dover Publications, 1976), 161, 167; New York Public Library, 11, 14, 60, 128, 159; United Press International, 119; *Vertebrate Paleontology*, by Alfred S. Romer (Berkeley, California: University of California Press, 1933), 4; Marie T. Womack/International Society of Cryptozoology; 98

Monster Dinosaur
Copyright © 1983 by Daniel Cohen
All rights reserved. No part of this book may be used or reproduced in any manner whatsoever without written permission except in the case of brief quotations embodied in critical articles and reviews. Printed in the United States of America. For information address J.B. Lippincott Junior Books, 10 East 53rd Street, New York, N.Y. 10022. Published simultaneously in Canada by Fitzhenry & Whiteside, Limited, Toronto.

Library of Congress Cataloging in Publication Data
Cohen, Daniel
  Monster dinosaur.
  Summary: An informal potpourri of facts, theories, and lore about dinosaurs and the people who study them.
    1. Dinosaurs—Juvenile literature.–[1. Dinosaurs]
  I. Title.
  QE862.D5C626–1983   567.9'1   82-48460
  ISBN 0-397-31953-3
  ISBN 0-397-31954-1 (lib. bdg.)

Designed by Al Cetta
1 2 3 4 5 6 7 8 9 10
First Edition

To the Walker Museum

Contents

MONSTER DINOSAUR

CHAPTER 1

Confessions of a Dinosaurophile

I can't remember when I first became fascinated by dinosaurs. I can't remember any time when I was *not* fascinated by those marvelous monsters. It's possible that my first extended exposure to dinosaurs came from reading the "prehistoric" comic strip "Alley Oop." "Alley Oop" ran in the *Chicago Tribune*. My parents never bought the *Tribune*, but an uncle who worked on a newspaper delivery truck usually brought me the Sunday comics (on Thursday!) from all of the papers, so at least I saw the color install-ment each week. I knew what was going to happen before any other kid on the block did. Alley Oop's "prehistoric" world of cavemen and dinosaurs was always more interesting to me than Buck Rogers' world of the future.

This interest in the prehistoric world had grown into something of an obsession by the time I was about eleven and discovered the Walker Museum. We lived on the South Side of Chicago, near the campus of the University of Chicago. On the campus was the Oriental Institute, an archeological museum with excellent exhibits of Egyptian and other Middle Eastern antiquities. Housed in an adjoining building was the Walker Museum, a museum of paleontology. Paleontology is the study of fossils.

While the Oriental Institute usually had many visitors each day, and was certainly well lighted and guarded, I'm not sure the Walker was ever even open to the public. I got in through a side door from the Oriental Institute. I think the door was supposed to be kept locked, but it rarely was. The Walker Museum's main lights were never on, and all the illumination came from light through the windows, and from the few naked bulbs above the exit signs and on the staircase. There were no visitors, no guards, nobody. I must have been in the Walker fifty times without ever seeing another living soul. Once I thought I heard someone moving around in one of the offices upstairs, and that scared me so badly that I ran out of the place. Every other time it was just me and the bones in the semidarkness. Just being there gave me an exhilarating feeling of awe and terror.

The Walker was not a large museum, and it didn't have any of the really big dinosaur skeletons. But one exhibit I do remember particularly well was a leg bone from one of the big dinosaurs, perhaps a brontosaur. The bone was nearly as big as I was. It was just set out on a base, not encased in glass. You could reach out and touch it, which I did repeatedly—and it always gave me a tingling sensation. To actually touch something that had once been part of a dinosaur was quite an extraordinary experience!

The really big dinosaurs were on exhibit at the Field Museum of Natural History, just a half-hour train ride from where I lived. Of course, you couldn't get near enough to touch the exhibits at the Field Museum. If you had tried, you probably would have been thrown out. But they were marvelous anyway. And almost as exciting as the reconstructed *Tyrannosaurus* were the Charles R. Knight murals showing life in the days of the dinosaurs. These murals covered the walls of the dinosaur hall. Knight's reconstructions were justly world famous, and as I stared at them, I knew that this was the way the prehistoric world had to have looked.

My favorite book in those days was *Vertebrate Paleontology* by Alfred S. Romer of Harvard University. It was a thick, seven-hundred-page volume that contained passages like this:

> The body was rather massively built. The neck vertebrae were opisthocoelous, and extra articulations, in addition to the normal zygapophyses, tended to add to

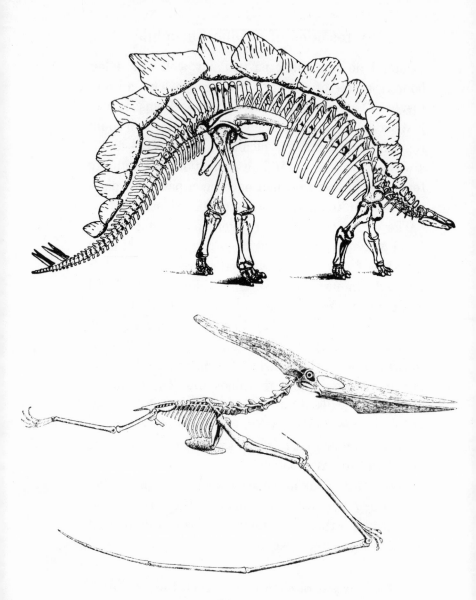

Two drawings from Romer's *Vertebrate Paleontology*. Above, stegosaur; below, pterosaur.

the strength of the backbone. The hind legs of the
creature were stout and only moderately long, and the
femur was somewhat longer than the tibia. The meta-
tarsals were rather short. . . .

That was pretty heavy going, particularly for someone who generally preferred Captain Marvel to
Charles Dickens. Still, I struggled gamely through it,
not understanding a tenth of what I read. What I
really liked were the pictures of dinosaur skeletons.
I cherished the book, and I still have it today.

Was I a weird kid?

I don't really think so. I think that at one time or
another in their lives most kids are fascinated by dinosaurs. I certainly wasn't the only one who stood for
hours gaping at the Charles R. Knight murals in the
Field Museum.

Book publishers often say that dinosaur books always sell because kids love dinosaurs. In 1980, Dr.
John E. Schowalter of Yale University tried to find
out why. One of the things he noticed is that interest
in dinosaurs starts young. He said, "I've always been
struck by the number of three- to five-year-old kids
who can't even pronounce the names of their class-
mates but know the names, sizes, habits, and number
of bones of several dinosaurs. It's the first type of
factual information a child may know better than his
parents do."

According to Dr. Schowalter, "Dinosaurs offer

something better than comic-book heroes. They actually existed, but they no longer do, so there is both the distance necessary for fantasy and a body of knowledge that can be mastered."

Dr. Schowalter also said that the kids who were most interested in dinosaurs were usually the brightest ones in their class. Hearing that made me feel pretty good, and it should make all of you reading this book feel pretty good, too.

When I first became interested in dinosaurs, I didn't think about how people had come to know of the existence of the creatures in the first place. I somehow assumed that people had always known about dinosaurs. Actually, the discovery of the dinosaurs is a fairly recent event in the history of the human race. As recently as the 1820s no one knew for sure (and few even suspected) that such astonishing creatures had ever existed. The public found it very difficult to accept the idea that there were animals of *any* kind that no longer existed. And that such spectacular animals could have existed and then died out was quite inconceivable to most. The discovery of the dinosaurs came as something of a shock.

Another impression I had was that people had always thought that dinosaurs looked and acted just like the ones in the Charles R. Knight murals. Wrong again. The earliest reconstructions of dinosaurs look weird and even funny to us today. Though they were made by the best scientists of the day, they were completely inaccurate. It wasn't till the time of World War I that the general image of the dinosaur settled into what might be called the Charles R. Knight view.

Paleontology is by no means a large or lavishly funded field of science, particularly today. On a percentage basis, there are probably fewer paleontologists now than there were a century ago. The field attracts less money for research than other areas of scientific endeavor. Still, new finds are made and studied; new evidence piles up. But change comes more slowly to paleontology than to other fields, and for a long time there were no basic changes in our thinking about dinosaurs.

Within the last ten or fifteen years, however, the staid old field of paleontology has been thrust into the midst of an astonishing revolution. Some of the most fundamental ideas about dinosaurs have been strongly challenged. My old view of the world of the dinosaurs as something firmly established and essentially unchanging has been shattered. Ten years from now, the old Charles R. Knight murals may be completely out of date. So may many of our most cherished opinions about dinosaurs.

In the pages that follow, I am going to explore how our view of the dinosaur has changed since the time when we first recognized that such monstrous creatures existed. How many old and outdated notions about dinosaurs are *you* still carrying around? More than you suspect, I'll wager. But you will not be disappointed to discover that according to the latest theories, dinosaurs were even more awesome and terrible than you thought they were.

There is more to our fascination with dinosaurs than the strictly scientific study and interpretation of their fossil bones. There is what might be called the romantic quest for a living dinosaur. Despite what modern dinosaur hunters claim, it really *is* more of a romantic quest than a scientific one, for the chances that anyone will actually find a living dinosaur are very slim. And yet, there has recently been a small but interesting flicker of hope that perhaps, just perhaps, the legends of a surviving dinosaur may be true. Interest in finding a living dinosaur is keener now than it has been in half a century. I'll tell you how all that has come about.

And then, dinosaurs have not remained the exclusive property of scientists. Shortly after they were discovered they were taken up by writers, and later by filmmakers. The writers and filmmakers probably have had more to do with what the average person thinks about dinosaurs than the scientists have. I'll relate to you the literary and cinematic history of the dinosaur. And finally, we will examine the possibility that the dinosaur is responsible for the creation of humanity's greatest legend.

You see, there is a lot more to dinosaurs than their strange names and impressive statistics. I hope that you will enjoy this rather informal ramble through the science, history, lore, and art of the dinosaur. You may learn some things as well, but most of all I hope you'll have fun. I had fun writing this book, and in doing the research for it. I was, for a short time, transformed back into that kid standing in the semi-darkness of the Walker Museum touching the tibia of a *Brontosaurus* and experiencing a tingling sensation of terror and awe.

(Today the *Brontosaurus* is more properly called the *Apatosaurus*, but I have generally used the older and more familar name in this book.)

CHAPTER 2

Dinner in a Dinosaur

In nightmares you may have had the terrifying experience of becoming dinner for a dinosaur. You may even have fantasized killing a dinosaur, cutting it up into steaks, and dining on it. But I'll bet you've never considered dining *in* a dinosaur. Yet such a thing really happened once—not in a real dinosaur, of course, but in a model of one. Here is how the strange banquet all came about.

During the first half of the nineteenth century, a series of fossil finds led scientists to the astounding and unexpected conclusion that at one time the Earth had been inhabited by very large, very strange-looking creatures. The scientists called these creatures "dinosaurs." It was also discovered that at the time of the dinosaurs there were creatures nearly as large, and every bit as strange-looking, swimming around in the oceans or soaring through the skies.

These discoveries immediately captured the imagination of educated men and women throughout the world. Nowhere was the fascination with dinosaurs greater than in England, a nation that prided itself (with considerable justification) on its devotion to the sciences. Besides, many of the good early finds of dinosaur fossils were made in England, and the ma-

Early and wildly inaccurate conception of what dinosaurs looked like.

Late-nineteenth-century drawing of marine reptiles from the age of the dinosaurs. In the foreground is the fishlike *Ichthyosaurus*; in the background, the long-necked *Plesiosaurus.*

jority of the experts in the new and expanding field of dinosaurian studies were English. The world's fascination with dinosaurs really began in Victorian England.

In 1852, London's famed Crystal Palace, the largest iron-framed glass building ever constructed, and the centerpiece for the Great Exhibition of 1851, was to be dismantled and moved from the Exhibition site to a new location in the suburbs of London. At a place called Sydenham the celebrated building would be reconstructed; it was to become a museum for the arts and sciences.

Queen Victoria's consort, Prince Albert, was a man much interested in science. He had been the moving force behind the Great Exhibition itself, and now he involved himself deeply in the plans for the new museum. He suggested that it would be highly educational if the grounds around the Crystal Palace were decorated with reconstructions of some of the great creatures of past ages. Not only would these be educational—they would probably help attract the crowds. Sydenham was rather out of the way, and there would be a charge for admission to the grounds of the museum. A display of exotic creatures might help to make the project a paying proposition.

The task of making the reconstructions was placed in the hands of wildlife painter Benjamin Waterhouse Hawkins, who had worked on the original Great Exhibition. It was a very ambitious undertaking. An artificial six-acre lake was dug, and in it were placed three islands that were to be home to the "antediluvian monsters." At first Hawkins considered filling the islands with prehistoric mammals like the mastodon (which was fairly well known in 1852). But, as it happened, Hawkins had just been reading some papers on the newly discovered dinosaurs. These papers, written by the British zoologist Richard Owen, fas-

Cartoon from the early 1900s showing dinosaurs, the woolly mammoth, cave men and a host of other creatures inhabiting the same world.

cinated Hawkins. He immediately contacted Owen, who agreed to help with the Crystal Palace project. Together the two men decided to concentrate on building models of the dinosaurs. Hawkins said he was summoning, "from the abyss of time and from the depths of the Earth, those vast forms and gigantic beasts which the Almighty Creator designed with fitness to inhabit and precede us in possession of this part of the Earth called Great Britain."

Working under Owen's careful direction, Hawkins first made small scale models, and then life-size clay models that would serve as molds. The final figures were hollow, braced on the inside with iron, covered with stucco, and painted. They were heavy, the largest weighing up to thirty tons. They proved to be astonishingly durable.

Three different kinds of dinosaur were represented. There were two *Iguanodon*s, a *Hylaeosaurus*, and a *Megalosaurus*. (These were the only types of dinosaur known in Britain at the time.) There were also a number of ancient marine creatures—the mosasaur, the ichthyosaur, and several plesiosaurs. These creatures were placed either in the water or near it. A couple of giant pterodactyls surveyed the "prehistoric" scene from the top of an artificial cliff. In addition, there were some creatures that looked like giant toads and frogs, and others that resembled turtles with tusks, or long-nosed crocodiles. One of the islands was reserved for extinct mammals like the giant sloth and the Irish elk.

Unfortunately, Owen and Hawkins had gotten the shape of the dinosaurs all wrong, and later paleontologists have subjected the Crystal Palace restorations to much ridicule and scorn. But the later judgments are too harsh. Owen and Hawkins were doing the best they knew how, and they had only fragmentary remains to work with. Take the most famous of the dinosaurs known in the 1850s, the

Iguanodon. Its remains were first discovered in Britain by Gideon Mantell in 1822. *Iguanodon* was really the first dinosaur ever to be identified as such, and in 1852 far and away the best known. Yet all anyone possessed were fragmentary remains—mostly teeth. At that time no one had ever found a complete skeleton, or even the major portion of one.

The fossil teeth resembled the teeth of the modern iguana, and Mantell had named his discovery after that lizard. (The name *Iguanodon* means "iguana tooth.") Knowledge of dinosaurian anatomy was in its infancy in 1852. So, when Owen and Hawkins tried to figure out what the living *Iguanodon* had looked like, they naturally started with the modern iguana. But the fossils clearly showed that *Iguanodon* had been much larger than any living lizard. *Iguanodon* had been a heavy creature—something like a modern rhinoceros, Owen and Hawkins guessed. And so the *Iguanodon*s that were built for the Crystal Palace looked rather like crosses between a rhinoceros and a lizard. The creatures even had rhinolike horns on their noses. Later it was discovered that the bone taken to be this "horn" was really a thumb joint. But that was not the worst of it. We now know that *Iguanodon* did not have a thick body set on four stumpy legs, as Owen envisioned. It stood upright, or nearly so, and possessed large powerful back legs and small front legs. *Iguanodon* actually resembled a gigantic kangaroo more closely than either the iguana or the rhinoceros.

But it's probably a good thing Owen and Hawkins didn't know this, because if they had, there never could have been the famous dinner in the dinosaur. There wouldn't have been enough room—or if there had been, the table would have to have been set at a steep angle.

Since the Crystal Palace *Iguanodon* was agreeably level, on New Year's Eve, 1853, Hawkins had a banquet table put inside his partially completed model, and he entertained twenty-one of Great Britain's leading scientists and scholars at a dinner there. The seating was a bit cramped, but by all accounts the banquet was a splendid success. After the toasts were drunk, and the men of science climbed out of their dinosaur and, filled with good food and excellent port, made their way homeward, they must have felt like masters not only of this world, but of the world of ages past as well.

Victorian Englishmen were a self-confident lot. Certainly large segments of the public felt that the Crystal Palace dinosaurs were a grand triumph. Of the dinner, the *Quarterly Review* said, "Saurians and Pterodactyles all! Dreamed ye ever, in your ancient festivities, of a race to come, dwelling above your tombs . . . dining on your ghosts, called from the deep by their sorcerers?"

Drawing of Hawkins's dinner in a dinosaur that appeared in *The Illustrated London News* in 1853.

Sorcerers, that's what the scientists seemed to be, and their creations were monsters from before the flood of Noah.

On June 10, 1854, the newly restored Crystal Palace was officially opened at Sydenham, with Queen Victoria herself in attendance. In general, the Hawkins models were a great success, but there was one odd omission. The organizers of the museum had failed to put up signs telling visitors what the statues were supposed to represent, so visitors who had not purchased Owen's guidebook had no idea what they were looking at. Someone suggested that the monstrous creatures had been erected by a temperance society as a warning to all drinkers of what they would begin to see if they did not stop drinking.

Ultimately, the Hawkins–Owen models of dinosaurs were shown to be grossly in error. They don't even faintly resemble the dinosaurs as we now believe they looked. The Crystal Palace itself burned down in 1936. But the old dinosaur models and their "antediluvian" companions were unharmed, and they are still there in Sydenham on their "prehistoric" islands. The models are no longer a major tourist attraction, but if you ever get to London, they are well worth a visit, for they are eloquent testimony to what the earliest discoverers of dinosaurs thought the creatures looked like.

In the years that followed the American Civil War, interest in dinosaurs migrated to the United States, and for a time a sort of dinosaur mania gripped the nation. In New York City, the Board of Commissioners of Central Park got the idea that dinosaur restorations would not only be a popular attraction for the new park, but would also be of enormous educational value to the public. And who was the man to build these restorations? Why, none other than Waterhouse Hawkins, builder of the famed Crystal Palace dinosaurs and host for the dinner in the dinosaur.

In 1868, Hawkins was asked if he would "under-

Two reconstructions of the *Iguanodon:* early and incorrect four-legged version, and later, more nearly correct upright version.

take the resuscitation of a group of animals of the former periods of the American continent." He agreed, and began with great enthusiasm to visit all the museums in America, and to meet with all the leading figures of American paleontology. Within the year he had completed several models in his Central Park studio, and was hard at work on others. Why, you might wonder, have you never seen these models, or even heard of them? The answer to that question can be found in a rather sordid and murky tale of greed and ignorance.

At the time Hawkins was building his models, the real political power in New York City lay in the hands of one William Marcy Tweed, or "Boss" Tweed, of Tammany Hall. Tweed and his henchmen had been systematically defrauding the city for some time, and Tweed was not a man who had much sympathy for educational projects like a paleontological exhibit in Central Park. Education had a very low priority in Boss Tweed's scheme of things.

So, in 1870, Tweed managed to throw out the old Central Park commissioners and replace them with his own corrupt associates. Work on the paleontological exhibit was soon halted because, the new park commissioners said, it was costing too much money. The real reason was that there was no way for the corrupt politicians to make money on such a project.

Hawkins, however, apparently continued to work on his models. At any rate, he had completed a large number of them by the spring of 1871. Then real disaster struck. At Tweed's orders, a group of vandals broke into Hawkins' studio and smashed all the casts and models to bits with sledgehammers. The broken pieces were carted away and buried somewhere in the southern portion of Central Park, where, presumably, they remain today.

Poor Hawkins stood by helplessly. What could he do? The models weren't really his—he was building them for the city of New York. Hawkins was even taunted by the vandals, who told him he should not bother himself about dead animals, when there were so many living ones to care for.

The sheer wanton destructiveness of this act was really uncharacteristic of Tweed. If he didn't like the models, he could doubtless have turned a profit on them by selling them to the Smithsonian Institution or some other museum, which would have been glad to have the creations of Waterhouse Hawkins gracing its halls. But Tweed chose to destroy the models and take the loss. Clearly Tweed hated the whole dinosaur project; what is not so clear is why. He probably disliked the park commissioners who had first developed the project, because they were his political opponents. And he probably didn't like Waterhouse Hawkins, because Hawkins was an Englishman. In the end, he probably didn't like dinosaurs, and perhaps he did not even believe in them. Paleontologist Adrian J. Desmond has suggested that Tweed's hatred may have

What Waterhouse Hawkins's "Paleozoic Museum" in Central Park would have looked like if it had ever been built. Reconstructions are a mixture of dinosaurs and various extinct mammals that lived long after the dinosaurs.

stemmed from a deep religious bigotry. Desmond said, "Certainly he appeared to be skeptical of the great antiquity of dinosaurs themselves, referring to Hawkins' models as 'specimens of animals *alleged* to be of the pre-Adamite period.'"

If only the destruction of Hawkins' models had been delayed for a few more months! By that time Boss Tweed himself would have been destroyed. Repeated exposures of the fraud and corruption of the Tweed Ring finally had their effect—Tweed was arrested and sent to jail. Ultimately he escaped and fled to Cuba, but he was rearrested and returned to a New York jail, and there, in 1878, he died. Those who had hired Hawkins in the first place sat on the park board again. But it was too late.

Hawkins left New York City for the relative quiet of the College of New Jersey at Princeton. After resting his shattered nerves for a few months, he began working on dinosaurs again, doing a series of seventeen huge paintings of prehistoric scenes with dinosaurs. He also made a model of a *Hadrosaurus* that stood for many years in front of the National Museum in Washington, D.C.

Despite the opposition of the likes of Boss Tweed, dinosaurs became extremely popular in the United States during the latter half of the nineteenth century. And the United States really became the center of dinosaur studies in the world. The reasons for this were both economic and geological.

The United States was becoming an increasingly wealthy nation. It had the money to finance the search for dinosaur fossils, and the individuals and the institutions to study and display the fossils properly. And the more popular dinosaurs became, the more financial backing paleontological research attracted.

The geological reasons may have been even more important. Europe is not particularly well suited for the preservation and recovery of fossils. Most European finds were either fragmentary or accidental, or the discoveries were made as the result of deep mining operations. The British, who were so inordinately proud of the dinosaurs found in their native soil, in fact possessed only a relative handful of fossils. They had just been the first to recognize the significance of the finds.

Parts of Asia and Africa are rich in fossils, but in the nineteenth century these places were too remote from the centers of scientific investigation to come under much scrutiny. America, with its growing scientific community and interest in science, was another matter.

The American West, particularly the broad band of arid lands that stretches from Mexico right up to Canada, is an area well suited for the preservation of fossils. By the 1800s, erosion caused by strong winds and the infrequent but heavy rains had exposed many of these fossils to view. They were simply lying around on the ground for anyone to see. Yet, for a long time, few saw or cared. Then, as the West became more accessible, and as knowledge of dinosaurs grew, a sort of "Bone Rush" began. It wasn't quite as intense and dramatic as the Gold Rush, which sent thousands scurrying across the continent to California and led to many gunfights over the best gold-bearing lands. Still, the search for dinosaur bones did have its moments of intrigue and drama.

Most of the intrigue and drama was provided by two men, Edward Drinker Cope and Othniel Charles

Marsh. Cope and Marsh were two of America's three leading paleontologists during the late nineteenth century. (The third was Joseph Leidy, who was somewhat older than Cope and Marsh, and a shy, noncombative individual.)

Anyone who thinks that science is a stately, dignified, and objective search for the truth need only consider the careers of Cope and Marsh. Scientific inquiry is often—even usually—riddled with jealousy, hatred, underhandedness, and even downright fraud. Scientists are, after all, human, just like the rest of us. That truth generally does emerge from this emotional morass is the glory of the scientific method.

Cope and Marsh were perhaps a little *more* human than most scientists. Cope was born in 1840 into a wealthy Philadelphia Quaker household. As a boy he was brilliant, energetic, and (in spite of his family's Quaker pacifism) very belligerent. By the age of eighteen he was challenging his scientific elders at the Philadelphia Academy of Natural Sciences on some fine points of biological classification.

During his lifetime, Cope turned out well over a thousand scientific papers and books on a staggering variety of subjects. But he was a bit too anxious to claim the glory of publishing a discovery *first*, so he often hurried. And so, while he did make great discoveries, he also made serious errors. The trouble was that Cope hated to admit that he had made a mistake—in fact, he rarely did. His usual reaction was to blow up at the person who had pointed the error out. On at least one occasion he finished a discussion at a meeting of the American Philosophical Society with a fistfight. "If you think my eye is black, you ought to see Frazer [his opponent] this morning!" Cope proudly told an associate the day after the fight.

Othniel Charles Marsh was nine years older than Cope, and in many respects a different sort of character. Cope had been precocious; Marsh was a slow starter. Marsh was born poor, and he was an indifferent student as a boy. Some have said that Marsh went into science simply to get money out of his rich uncle. His uncle, George Peabody, was indeed very, very rich, and he did have a reputation for supporting scientific endeavors.

Peabody sent Marsh through Yale and thought his money well spent, for the youth turned into a first-rate student who showed a real talent for paleontology. Peabody continued to support his nephew, and when he died he left Marsh well provided for. Marsh had persuaded Peabody to settle a huge sum of money on Yale for the construction of a natural history museum, and, in gratitude, Yale made O. C. Marsh the first professor of paleontology in America.

Marsh's scientific publications were not as numerous or as brilliant as Cope's. His research was slow, careful, limited—but he didn't often make mistakes. However, Marsh resembled Cope in one critical way—he, too, had an enormous ego, and did not wish to stand in anyone's shadow. While he was often charming to those he wished to impress, he could also be selfish, sneaky, underhanded, and downright mean.

Both men entered the expanding and newly glamorous field of paleontology at about the same time, and I suppose a clash was inevitable. The flash point was reached in a dispute over an *Elasmosaurus* skeleton.

An *Elasmosaurus* is a spectacular long-necked plesiosaur, and Cope had restored the skeleton of one for the Philadelphia Academy. He was terribly proud of it, but to the careful Marsh it looked just a bit too spectacular, and when he examined it closely he realized that Cope had gotten the whole thing wrong—he had put the head at the end of the tail. When Marsh mentioned this error to Cope, perhaps none too gently, Cope exploded and insisted that he knew one end of an *Elasmosaurus* from the other. He was wrong, though he didn't want to admit it, and he never forgave Marsh. "He has since been my bitter enemy," said Marsh.

Though he would not admit his error openly, Cope knew he was wrong, and he was deeply embarrassed. He tried to buy up, at his own expense, all the copies of the paper that described his erroneous restoration. Marsh refused to sell the two copies he owned.

What followed has been called the Battle of the Bones, the Great Fossil Feud, and Dinosaur Wars. It might also be called the Clash of the Names. For the paleontologist, names are very important. The first person to describe a new species in a scientific paper gets to give it a Latin scientific name. This is a highly prized honor, and there have always been disputes over who has the right to name what.

With every new discovery, Cope would rush headlong into print, in order to give the new creature a name. Marsh would retaliate by claiming that he (or someone else) had already described the beast under a different name. Both men were guilty of claiming as their own creatures that had been discovered by others. The net result was confusion, and one dinosaur might wind up with several different names.

Cope called one of his discoveries *Laelaps*. Marsh pointed out that the name had already been used for at least two other creatures. Marsh himself changed Cope's *Laelaps* to *Dryptosaurus*. Cope ignored the change, but not the challenge. Marsh had discovered a truly gigantic dinosaur he called *Titanosaurus*, or "titanic lizard." Cope searched through the literature and found that the name *Titanosaurus* had already been used. He told Marsh to find another name. This was not a high level of scientific debate.

Since Cope and Marsh were at the time among the world's leading paleontologists, and since they had access to the richest and most productive fossil beds in the world, this confusion of names became enormous. Years later, Henry Fairfield Osborn of the

American Museum of Natural History complained, "It has been the painful duty of Professor [William Berryman] Scott and myself to devote thirty of the best years of our lives to trying to straighten out this nomenclatural chaos."

The nature of the struggle can be illustrated by this incident. In 1872, Cope found fragmentary remains of three different types of dinosaur in the Washakie Basin in Wyoming, but he feared that Marsh would somehow preempt his find. There was no time to lose, so he sent the secretary of the American Philosophical Society a telegram that read:

I HAVE DISCOVERED IN SOUTHERN WYOMING THE FOLLOWING SPECIES COLON LOXOLOPHODON COPE STOP INCISOR ONE TUSK CANINE NONE SEMICOLON PREMOLARS FOUR COMMA WITH ONE CRESCENT AND INNER TUBERCLE SEMICOLON MOLARS TWO SEMICOLON SIZE GIGANTIC STOP DASH DICORNUTUS SEMICOLON HORNS TRIPEDRAL CYLINDRIC SEMICOLON NASALS WITH SHORT CONVEX LOBES STOP DASH BIFURCATUS COMMA NASALS WITH LONG SPATULATE LOBES STOP DASH EXPRESSICORNS COMMA HORNS COMPRESSED AND ACUMINATE.

The secretary of the American Philosophical Society may have been able to make some sense out of all of that, but it certainly must have confused the poor telegraph operator, who substituted Lefalophodon for Loxolophodon. Indeed, no one seems to have been paying very close attention, for the error found its way into several later works on paleontology.

In the early years of the nineteenth century, it was the practice of people who found interesting fossils to send them on to a leading scientist or scientific institution, gratis. There was no money to be made in this sort of science; there was only the desire to advance human knowledge. But as the romance of paleontology grew, all that changed. Now interesting fossils were not only objects of scientific interest, they were symbols of prestige for individuals, institutions, and even whole nations. Money could be had for fossils, and the prices went up all the time. Cope and Marsh, both independently wealthy men, were reasonably well situated to engage in bidding wars for fossils (though in this respect Marsh, who had the larger personal fortune, had the upper hand).

By 1877, the pair had been sniping at each other in print and in person for some years. Then they got the opportunity to really fight it out. In March 1877, a teacher and amateur fossil hunter named Arthur Lakes stumbled across some gigantic bones near the town of Morrison, Colorado. He wrote of his discovery to Marsh, who failed to reply. While waiting in vain for an answer from Marsh, Lakes thoroughly explored the territory, and made even more remarkable discoveries. He wrote an even more enthusiastic letter to Marsh, and still he received no reply. There was a third letter, and a fourth, each describing successively greater discoveries. Lakes even packed up about a ton of dinosaur bones and sent them to Marsh at New Haven, Connecticut—and still Marsh did nothing.

Then Arthur Lakes did the one thing that was sure to stimulate Marsh to action—he wrote of his discoveries to Cope, and even sent him some specimens. The instant Marsh heard of this, he cabled Lakes in an attempt to prevent him from sending any more material to his rival. He also cabled one of his field collectors to strike a deal with the schoolteacher immediately. This was done.

Cope, in his usual haste, was already preparing a paper describing the specimens that Lakes had sent him when he received a devastating letter from Lakes. This informed him that Marsh had purchased all of the specimens, and that he should send the fossils directly on to Marsh. Cope's fury can only be imagined.

Score one for Marsh, but Cope was to have his day. It seems that another schoolteacher, O. W. Lucas, was collecting plants near Canon City, Colorado, at about this same time. He, too, stumbled upon giant bones, and his first reaction was to write to Cope. Cope did not delay. He had his representatives contact Lucas at once and arrange to buy the bones.

Now it was Marsh's turn to be upset. His agents visited the site of Lucas's discovery, which was about one hundred miles to the south of Lakes' Morrison find. The agents reported that the bones at Canon City were bigger, and in a better state of preservation. Lucas seemed unhappy with the arrangements he had concluded with Cope, and Marsh's agents tried to buy him out. But the schoolteacher stuck loyally by his agreement, and soon crates of bones were on their way to Cope in Philadelphia. There followed a stream of scientific papers describing the discoveries, from Cope's energetic pen.

Then fortune again favored O. C. Marsh. He received a letter from two men informing him that they had found some gigantic bones in Wyoming, and that since Marsh was "well known as an enthusiastic geologist and a man of means, both of which we are desirous of finding—more especially the latter," they were offering to sell him the bones. Marsh, reacting quickly this time, sent one of his trusted associates, Samuel Wendell Williston, to check into the offer.

Williston found that the letter writers were a couple of railroad men who worked for the Union Pacific. They had found their fossils at Como Bluff in southern Wyoming. Williston was ecstatic. He wrote that the bones "extend for seven miles and are by the ton. . . . The bones are very thick, well preserved, and easy to get out." Later, he said that "Canon City and

Morrison are simply nowhere in comparison with this locality, as regards perfection, accessibility, and quantity."

Marsh immediately signed up the railroad men to work for him, and he stipulated that they were to do their best to keep other collectors out of the area, though exactly how they were to do this, Marsh did not say. The laws regarding the ownership of fossil bones found on public lands were by no means clear, and later both Cope and Marsh were to be charged with stealing fossils.

Parties in the pay of Cope or Marsh were always snooping around each other's diggings. Cope, who spent far more time actually out in the field than Marsh did, once appeared at Marsh's diggings in disguise, though the disguise was soon penetrated. Marsh's associates were astounded by the man's personal charm. When not actually engaged in combat, Cope could be excellent company, Arthur Lakes wrote in his journal. "The *monstrum horrendum* Cope has been and gone, and I must say that what I saw of him I liked very much. His manner is so affable, and his conversation very agreeable. I only wish I could feel sure he had a sound reputation for honesty."

There are stories of parties of Cope and Marsh diggers actually shooting at each other, but these are probably exaggerations. The legend of the monumental Cope–Marsh struggle has grown over the years.

Mostly, the rival parties seem to have contented themselves with filching fossils from each other's diggings and with trying to buy off each other's workers. However, in one way the feuding did go too far. When they abandoned a site, the workmen for one side would often break up whatever fossils remained in order to keep the other side from obtaining anything of value. Part of America's fossil record was thus destroyed forever.

The Como Bluff site did turn out to be the richest in the bones of giant dinosaurs. Marsh kept diggers working there until 1889. He got the best of Cope when it came to the discovery of the fossils of really large dinosaurs. But Cope had his own successes, particularly in the excavation of the strange and spectacular duckbilled dinosaurs.

Cope was finally brought down by money, or rather the lack of it. He had been left a considerable fortune, but his fossil-hunting activities were expensive. Hoping to swell his fortune (and perhaps to compete more successfully with the wealthier Marsh), Cope invested heavily in speculative Western mining stocks—and he lost. He was left broke, and he had to pass up a number of excellent opportunities to explore new fossil finds. He was reduced to living on a small income provided by the Philadelphia Academy of Natural Sciences, the institution whose collection he had done so much to enrich. Cope spent his last years in a small rented house in Philadelphia that was crammed, floor to ceiling, with bones and papers. When he fell ill, he put off treatment until it was too late. Edward Drinker Cope died in April of 1897.

Marsh seemed to move from one success to another, collecting flocks of honors along the way. But the financial strain of fossil hunting was a little too much even for a man of his considerable wealth. In the end, Marsh accepted a salary from Yale. He had previously refused to take one because he hadn't needed it, and had felt that accepting payment from any institution would limit his independence.

Marsh had other problems as well. He had formed a close alliance with the U.S. Geological Survey, which had given him the chance to excavate in some Western areas that might otherwise have been closed to him. Many Western congressmen bitterly resented the conservation-minded Geological Survey, and they mobilized to break its power. In Congress, they brought up Marsh's paleontological activities and ridiculed some of his findings as examples of wasteful foolishness. The argument worked, and the Geological Survey's appropriations were severely cut. Since Marsh had depended heavily on the support of the Geological Survey, its decline hurt his work.

O. C. Marsh died in 1899. With his death the Great Fossil Feud officially ended—though, in fact, years before either of them died Cope and Marsh seemed to grow weary of the struggle, and stopped seeking confrontations. The great romantic era of freebooting American fossil hunting also died. Today, most fossil hunting is carried out by institutions, not individuals, and it is bounded by a host of rules and laws. It's not that controversies and conflicts don't arise—they do. But they cannot be as personal, bitter, and public as the monumental fights between Cope and Marsh were.

Today, opinion is divided as to whether the Cope–Marsh feud was good or bad for the dinosaurs. Certainly a great deal of time and effort was wasted by both men. Excavations may have been carried out in careless haste, and each man destroyed fossils in order to keep them out of the hands of the other. Certainly no one needed the "nomenclatural chaos" that Cope and Marsh created when they insisted upon calling dinosaurs by different names. But there are those who believe that, on balance, the rivalry was a good thing. It spurred Cope and Marsh on to ever greater exertions (and expenditures). In no other way could so much have been accomplished so quickly.

It is certain that before these two quarrelsome fellows had retired from active combat, our knowledge of dinosaurs had grown a great deal. Between them, Cope and Marsh discovered and popularized such dinosaurs as the huge *Allosaurus*, the strangely armored *Stegosaurus*, the nightmarishly horned plant eater *Triceratops*, and, perhaps most famous of all,

Our view of dinosaurs changes all the time. Not only does the old *Brontosaurus* have a new name, *Apatosaurus*, but it has a new head as well. After reexamining the records of original excavations, scientists at the Carnegie Museum of Natural History decided that the creature had a long-snouted skull, rather than a short-snouted one. The short-snouted skull, it seems, belongs to another dinosaur, *Camarasaurus*.

the gigantic dinosaurs *Brontosaurus* and *Diplodocus.*

People no longer had to depend on Waterhouse Hawkins' imaginative reconstructions for their ideas of dinosaurs. They could go to a museum and see the fossil bones themselves—and this tangible link with the fantastic creatures of the past was more impressive than any clay and plaster reconstruction. The fossils made the dinosaurs real to the general public. People flocked to see them—and they still do. (The dinosaur bones collected by Marsh are now on display at Yale and at the National Museum in Washington, D.C. The bulk of Cope's collection can be found in the halls of the American Museum of Natural History in New York City.)

Cope's and Marsh's dramatic discoveries, coupled with their publicity-grabbing fights, made "dinosaur" a household word in America. Because of their work, the image of the dinosaur as a particular kind of creature became firmly fixed in our minds.

And now, after about a century, we may have to change that image radically.

CHAPTER 3

A New Image for
the Dinosaur

If you were paying very close attention while you were reading the last chapter, you might have noticed that I never once referred to dinosaurs as reptiles. Nor did I call the time in which the dinosaurs lived "The Age of Reptiles." That was not an oversight— it was deliberate omission.

For over a century, both the general public and the scientific community have simply assumed that dinosaurs were reptiles. (The very name "dinosaur" means "terrible lizard." Richard Owens coined the term in 1842.) Now it turns out that this piece of common knowledge, like so many other things that "everyone knows," may be wrong. Today it is being said by some scientists that dinosaurs are—well, dinosaurs, a class unto themselves, no more closely related to the crocodile and the python than to the lion or the horse. Not everyone agrees, and the question of whether dinosaurs are reptiles or something else is far from settled. It may never be settled. What's interesting is that the question has arisen at all. The idea of dinosaurs as non-reptiles is revolutionary.

Even if it is finally decided that dinosaurs *were* reptiles, there can be no disputing that they were very extraordinary reptiles, not at all like your average turtle or iguana. For one thing, many dinosaurs were so huge. But size is not the only way in which the dinosaurs were different from today's reptiles.

The idea of dinosaurs as reptiles has greatly influenced our image of the dinosaurs. Since modern reptiles are slow and stupid, at least when compared with mammals, we have assumed that the dinosaurs must have been slow and stupid, too. Since we are mammals, that view must be regarded as an expression of barefaced mammalian chauvinism, a way of flaunting our superiority to the dinosaurs.

Dinosaurs were originally classified as reptiles because the best evidence available at the time indicated that that was what they were. Many anatomical features of dinosaurs do closely resemble those of modern reptiles. Remember, the first clearly identified dinosaur fossils were the teeth of the *Iguanodon*, so named because the teeth looked like the teeth of the modern iguana. Then there is the undoubted fact that dinosaurs laid eggs—and modern reptiles lay eggs, too. All in all, scientists saw no good reason *not* to classify dinosaurs as reptiles. Still, there were some nagging problems—problems that seemed only to deepen as new discoveries were made.

While fossil bones can tell us a lot about the structure of an animal, there is a lot that the bones cannot tell us. They cannot, for example, tell us with any certainty whether a creature was cold-blooded or warm-blooded.

The description of an animal as "cold-blooded" or "warm-blooded" can be a bit misleading. The crucial difference is not in the actual temperature of the blood at any given moment. Rather, the difference lies in whether or not a creature maintains a constant body temperature by generating its own internal body heat.

Creatures that do maintain a constant body temperature are called warm-blooded; but endothermic, "internally heated," is a more accurate description. Mammals and birds are endothermic. Human beings are mammals, and our body temperature remains at a fairly constant 98.6 degrees Fahrenheit. If it varies just a few degrees—for example, if it rises to 102 degrees—then we know that something is wrong. If our temperature drops just a few degrees and stays down over an extended period, we will die.

Cold-blooded creatures, on the other hand, lack internal temperature regulation. Their body temperature is controlled by the temperature of their environment. They are ectothermic—their body heat is externally controlled. Reptiles are ectothermic.

You have probably seen a lizard or a turtle sunning itself. The creature is not trying to get a suntan; it is warming its body, for only when its body has warmed up sufficiently can the reptile become active. Most reptiles are not active at night when there is no sun, and if they live in temperate climates, they hibernate in the winter.

Reptiles, like humans, can freeze or overheat. But ectothermic creatures can tolerate greater changes in body temperature than mammals and birds can.

Reptiles are capable of short bursts of great activity. (Startle a small snake or lizard and see how fast it can move.) But, in general, reptiles are much less active than either mammals or birds. They are not built for constant activity. Just look at the way the legs of a lizard or a crocodile are set. They sprawl; they are short and set far apart. And the body is slung low to the ground. When a lizard or crocodile is finished running or walking, all it has to do is flop down on its belly in order to rest. And that is the position in which it spends most of its time. The larger the reptile, the more slowly and less frequently it moves. While a small lizard can run (for a brief time) with surprising speed, a large crocodile cannot. Visitors watching the giant tortoises at the zoo often wonder whether the things are dead or alive.

If dinosaurs were the largest reptiles the world has

ever known, it follows that they should also have been the slowest. As reptiles, these giants should have spent the bulk of their time lying around on their bellies sunning themselves.

However, as scientists pieced together more and more dinosaur skeletons, it became apparent that, unlike modern lizards, dinosaurs were *not* built for lying around on their bellies sunning themselves. It seemed that most dinosaurs walked, ran, or perhaps even jumped about on two large, extremely strong back legs. And not only that. It seemed that dinosaurs might have been fairly active a good bit of the time.

Paleontologist Lawrence Lambe first described the fossils of the carnivorous *Gorgosaurus* back in 1913. This dinosaur was a huge beast, some twenty-nine feet long from nose to tail, and probably standing eleven feet high. Lambe, who assumed that *Gor-*

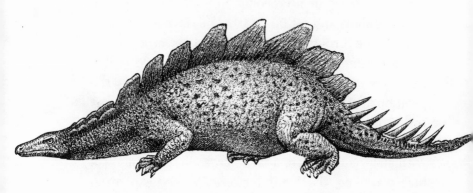

The "creeping *Stegosaurus*"—a dinosaur reconstructed on a lizardlike model.

gosaurus was a reptile, was convinced that the monster was a sluggish creature that spent most of its
time stretched out flat on the earth, moving only when
it was desperately hungry. Even then, said Lambe,
Gorgosaurus did not pursue prey—it was a scavenger, not a hunter. In Lambe's view, the creature
feasted on the carcasses of the gigantic plant-eating
dinosaurs that lived and died in such abundance.
There would have been so many carcasses available,
said Lambe, that even a slow-moving *Gorgosaurus*
would have been able to find enough to eat without
much trouble.

Though most paleontologists agreed that dinosaurs
were reptiles, they did not go along with Lambe's
extreme views about their inability to get around
quickly. The gigantic meat eaters like *Gorgosaurus*,
Tyrannosaurus, and *Allosaurus* just didn't look like
slow-moving scavengers. Scavengers don't need the
powerful jaws and enormous teeth of these dinosaurs
—these are the jaws and teeth of active predators.
Scavengers don't need the immensely powerful legs
of the carnivorous dinosaurs. After all, a scavenger's
prey is not going anywhere and will not fight back.
No, these are the jaws, teeth, and legs of animals that
had to chase and kill their food.

In 1938, an expedition from the American Museum
of Natural History uncovered some very dramatic
dinosaur tracks about eighty miles southwest of Fort
Worth, Texas, at Glen Rose. Dinosaur tracks had

been found before, but these were unusual because there was not just one set of tracks—there were two. The first tracks were those of a plant-eating dinosaur, probably a small brontosaur. The second tracks were a set of the three-toed prints of a carnivore. It looked as if the carnivorous dinosaur had been pursuing the smaller herbivore!

The end of the chase (if chase it was) is unknown, for the footprints disappeared at a point where the creatures stepped from mud to hard rock, where they left no prints. So, the Glen Rose tracks don't "prove" anything. But the discovery had a tremendous impact on both the scientific community and the general public. It supported what most people, scientist and layman alike, already believed—that the carnivorous dinosaurs were active and dangerous killers rather than sluggish and cowardly scavengers.

Paleontologist Adrian Desmond observed that "There plainly was a certain amount of doublethink going on. On the one hand, today's reptiles were recognized as possessing severe handicaps when it came to sustaining any sort of activity. Yet yesterday's glorified reptiles were capable of the most extraordinary feats. The paradox was only recognized as such by a few. . . ."

One way of getting around this paradox—or at least partway around—was to assume that while the dinosaurs were active, they weren't all *that* active. *Tyrannosaurus* and *Gorgosaurus* might have pursued their prey, but not at any great speed. They might have survived only because their prey— *Triceratops*, the duckbilled dinosaurs, and the like— were slower still. One imagines the chase and final kill taking place in lumbering slow motion.

Is that the way it happened? Or is it possible that predators and prey weren't really slow? Maybe they weren't slow because they weren't really reptiles? I'll get back to that rather startling possibility a little later on.

In addition to being slow when compared with mammals, reptiles are stupid. If dinosaurs were super reptiles in size, they were also (we thought) even stupider than their modern reptilian counterparts. They seemed to be hardly more than giant automations, with an extremely limited range of responses.

Most dinosaurs did have tiny brains, particularly compared with the enormous size of their bodies. The classic example of small-brained dinosaurian stupidity is the heavily armored *Stegosaurus*. Though it weighed as much as an elephant, its brain was the size of a walnut, and weighed about two and a half ounces! A brain of that size would hardly seem large enough to control the creature's enormous body.

Interestingly, *Stegosaurus*'s nervous system appears to have had some special adaptations. There was a bulge in the animal's spinal cord where it passed through the pelvis. This bulge was about twenty times as large as the brain itself. A fable arose: The story ran that *Stegosaurus* really had two brains, one in the head and one near the tail. In 1912, this fable inspired Bert Leston Taylor, a columnist for the *Chicago Tribune*, to compose a bit of satirical doggerel verse about dinosaurs. It turned out to be the most famous and influential piece of poetry ever written about the poor creatures. It goes like this:

> Behold the mighty dinosaur,
>   Famous in prehistoric lore,
> Not only for his power and strength
>   But for his intellectual length.
> You will observe by these remains
>   The creature had two sets of brains—
> One in his head (the usual place),
>   The other in his spinal base.
> Thus he could reason "*a priori*"
>   As well as "*a posteriori*."
> No problem bothered him a bit;
>   He made both head and tail of it.
>
> So wise was he, so wise and solemn,
>   Each thought filled just a spinal column.
> If one brain found the pressure strong
>   It passed a few ideas along.
> If something slipped his forward mind
>   'Twas rescued by the one behind.
> And if in error he was caught
>   He had a saving afterthought.
> As he thought twice before he spoke,
>   He had no judgment to revoke.

Thus he could think without congestion
        Upon both sides of every question.
Oh gaze upon this model beast:
        Defunct ten million years at least!

Taylor had underestimated the time of the dinosaurs' extinction by over fifty million years. And he was, of course, quite wrong about the "second brain." The enlargement may have served as a secondary control center for automatic movements of *Stegosaurus*'s hindquarters, but it was certainly no "*a posteriori*" brain.

Yet wrong as it was, Taylor's bit of doggerel became extremely popular, and indeed it is well remembered even today, seventy years after it was first published. How many serious poets have achieved that sort of fame?

Taylor's piece was popular because it expressed, in a rather humorous manner, a basic human attitude toward the dinosaurs. Here, says the poem, is this very large, very strange beast. But it's extinct. And we humans, who are not large and not strange-looking, are *not* extinct. Therefore, no matter how large the dinosaurs were, and no matter how many brains they might have had, we are superior, because we are still around.

For all of our fascination with the dinosaurs, we have come to hold them in contempt. We figure they were just too big, too slow, and too dumb to live, and that is why they died out—became extinct. The word "dinosaur," instead of evoking an image of terrifying power, has become almost an insult. Anything that's too large and inefficient may be referred to as a dinosaur. In the early 1970s, when the energy crisis struck the United States, the big, elaborate, low-gas-mileage cars that had once been so beloved by the American public were called dinosaurs. They had outlived their usefulness.

The trouble with our idea of the dinosaurs as big, slow, and stupid is that the fossil record shows—clearly—that the idea isn't right. In the first place, not all dinosaurs were large. Though the most spectacular and well-known of the dinosaurs are giants, smaller dinosaurs, some not much larger than a modern chicken, have been found. Many of these smaller dinosaurs were lightly built, and obviously would have been capable of considerable speed and agility. Then too, the skulls of these smaller dinosaurs show that not all dinosaurs had pea-sized brains. Many of the smaller dinosaurs had brains which were quite a respectable size in comparison to their bodies. (In some cases, the brain-to-body ratio approaches and even surpasses that of modern birds, and birds are considered to be rather intelligent creatures.)

Okay, you say. The dinosaurs weren't necessarily big, slow, and stupid. But they're extinct. Doesn't that show that *something* was wrong with them?

To that question, I'd have to say "no." It's true that

Compsognathus, one of the smallest and most agile of the dinosaurs, was about the size of a large chicken.

the dinosaurs have been "defunct ten million years at least"—actually closer to sixty-five million years. And no one knows why they died out. But you can bet that the reasons have nothing to do with dinosaur "unfitness." The dinosaurs were actually very successful animals. Prior to their extinction, they quite literally dominated the land for 140 million years. That is a significant period of time, even in the long history of the Earth.

Let's compare the record of our own species. Something vaguely resembling *Homo sapiens* has existed on this planet for three or four million years. We have been the dominant species for perhaps fifty thousand years. That is the merest eyeblink compared with the millions of years of dinosaurian dominance. When we have been around another hundred million years or so, we may then be able to begin to compare our success with that of the dinosaurs. Meanwhile, it is the grossest error for us to condemn the dinosaurs as somehow "unfit." That may make us feel superior, but it does not fit the known facts.

Of course, we are very interested in accounting for the extinction of the dinosaurs. (I'll discuss this topic in the next chapter.) But while we are working on that question, we must also try to account for the dinosaurs' success. If they were generally as sluggish, stupid, and oversized as common wisdom holds them to be, why were they around for so long? Why did they evolve in the first place?

Here we are back to the question of whether dinosaurs were reptiles.

Since the ripsnorting days of Cope and Marsh, the science of paleontology has settled into a state of somber respectability. Discovery has piled upon discovery. The fund of knowledge about dinosaurs has increased year by year. But there were no big changes in our basic ideas about dinosaurs until the 1960s. During that turbulent decade, a combination of new discoveries and a new way of looking at older finds led some scientists to advance the idea that dinosaurs were not reptiles at all.

One of the new discoveries, made in 1964, was an unusual carnivore called *Deinonychus*. This creature lived in what is now Montana in early Cretaceous times—that is, roughly 130 million years ago. It was not particularly large, for a dinosaur—it was a little over eight feet from nose to tail. Like other meat-eating dinosaurs, it was bipedal, with large, well-developed hind legs and small front legs adapted for grasping. A reconstruction of the remains showed that the creature moved with its head up, its body parallel to the ground, and its tail held out stiffly behind it. (It could not bend its tail at all.)

The consensus was that *Deinonychus* had the body of a runner. But perhaps the most extraordinary thing about *Deinonychus* were its feet. It ran on two toes. The third toe curved upward, and had been modified into a wicked-looking five-inch claw that could only have been used in slashing or tearing food or foe. Hence the dinosaur's name: *Deinonychus* means "terrible claw."

So what, you say. There are a lot of strange-looking dinosaurs. But try to imagine a living *Deinonychus* out hunting. To properly use the body it possessed, it must have run along at a considerable speed. It must have grasped its prey firmly in its front claws, holding the prey at arm's length. And then it must have slashed its hapless victim to death with the curved claw on its hind foot. And this it would have to do while standing on one leg!

Deinonychus, or "terrible claw," had to slash its prey with the claw on one hind foot while standing on the other.

This is not a creature that was sluggish, clumsy, or stupid. John Ostrom, the paleontologist who discovered *Deinonychus*, concluded that the creature was "anything but 'reptilian' in its behavior, responses, and way of life." He said it must have been a "fleet-footed, highly predaceous, extremely agile, and very active animal sensitive to many stimuli and quick in its responses." Ostrom also believed that the creature hunted in packs—another very unreptilian behavior pattern.

One of the first scientists to raise basic questions about the dinosaur–reptile identification was Dr. Robert T. Bakker of Johns Hopkins University, who made a study of the limb joints of some of the large horned dinosaurs, like *Triceratops*. He estimated that these dinosaurs could gallop at speeds of up to thirty miles per hour. That meant that the large carnivores that preyed on the likes of *Triceratops* had to be able to move quickly, too—not only to catch the plant eaters, but to avoid them. *Triceratops* was a ten-ton monster with a heavily armored head, enormous horns, and a tough, beaklike mouth. It would have been a formidable foe for even the largest and fiercest of the meat eaters. *Tyrannosaurus* possessed the weapons to kill *Triceratops*, but it would have been no easy task, and an impossible one if *Tyrannosaurus* was simply a pea-brained, slow-moving mass of flesh with big teeth.

It boils down to this. The dinosaurs would not have been able to move as rapidly and agilely as they apparently were capable of moving if they were just big lizards. So, by the mid-1960s, Bakker and a few others were presenting the heretical idea that perhaps dinosaurs were not reptiles at all—that perhaps they were in fact warm-blooded (endothermic). This might account not only for their speed, but for their success over millions of years.

Bakker and his associates took a close look at the fossil bones of some of the larger dinosaurs and found them rich in channels that once carried blood vessels. In this way, the fossil bones resembled the bones of modern mammals more closely than the bones of modern reptiles. And that wasn't all the scientists saw in the fossil record.

In order to sustain their body heat and higher activity levels, warm-blooded creatures must eat more than their cold-blooded counterparts—up to ten times more. There is no way fossil bones can tell us how many plants a herbivorous dinosaur consumed in a day or a week. But we can learn something from the ratio of predatory dinosaurs to the dinosaurs that presumably were their prey.

Since warm-blooded animals eat more than cold-blooded ones, it would take a larger population of prey to support one warm-blooded predator than to support one cold-blooded predator. In fact, the prey population would have to be extremely large, so that the warm-blooded predator, making many kills, would not just annihilate its own food supply.

Of present-day mammals, about 5 percent are predators, while about 45 percent of the living reptiles are predators. Bakker studied the predator–prey relationships in several fossil communities from the age of dinosaurs, and he found that the predator–prey ratio in those times resembled the modern mammalian ratio more closely than the reptilian.

An unusual find in Montana in 1978 added another bit of evidence to the case for the warm-blooded dinosaur. A local high school teacher ran across a tangle of small dinosaur bones. They were the remains of fifteen baby dinosaurs of a previously unknown species. The little dinosaurs had been killed suddenly, perhaps in a blast from a nearby volcano. The bones were found in and near an eggshell-littered nest— presumably the nest in which the babies had been hatched.

Finding dinosaur nests, eggs, and even baby dinosaurs is hardly an everyday occurrence, but it *had* happened before. However, there were other things about this particular find that made it seem significant.

The young dinosaurs were a new variety of duck-billed dinosaur. Thus, they were creatures adapted to feeding on swamp vegetation. Yet the nest had been built in the uplands, a considerable distance from the nearest swampy area. This nesting site must have been safer for the dinosaur eggs and newly hatched young. But these fifteen baby dinosaurs were *not* newly hatched. Their teeth showed considerable wear. They had probably hatched months before they died—yet they had stayed near the nest, and away from potential food sources in the swamps. How had they managed to eat?

Simple, says Dr. John R. Horner, a Princeton University paleontologist who studied the find. Their mother brought food to them.

Horner named the new variety of dinosaur *Maiasaurus*, or "maternal lizard." Now, this is something of a contradiction in terms, for modern lizards are not maternal, or paternal, either. They lay their eggs and then walk, crawl, or slither away.

The newly hatched young have to fend for themselves. One reptile, the python, does help incubate its eggs, but it provides no care after the young snakes are hatched.

Warm-blooded mammals and birds, however, do care for their young. Furthermore, birds, like dinosaurs, lay eggs. Mammals don't lay eggs, but there is a rare and curious group of mammallike creatures that do. They are the monotremes, and the best known is the duckbilled platypus of Australia. Scientists are not quite sure if monotremes are primitive mammals or an entirely separate group. They are warm-blooded, have fur, give milk, but their young are hatched from eggs.

Dr. Horner views the *Maiasaurus* find as strong evidence that dinosaurs were warm-blooded. And the feeding of the young is not only nonreptilian—it is considered an advanced behavioral trait. Horner told an interviewer for *The New York Times* that dinosaurs were a lot smarter than is generally thought.

A maternal dinosaur! The idea is staggering, and a long way from the image of the dinosaur as a lumbering, cold-blooded idiot.

"The data of the last five years constitute overwhelming evidence for warm-bloodedness," says Robert T. Bakker. That, however, is the opinion of a strong partisan. Not all paleontologists would agree.

While the new image of the dinosaur as a warm-blooded, active, and relatively intelligent creature appears to solve a host of problems, it does create some new ones. First, a little background. Let us look at the case of the giant plant eaters like *Brontosaurus* and *Diplodocus.* These famous dinosaurs, which belong to the suborder Sauropoda, were among the largest land animals that ever existed, at least as far as we know today. While most dinosaurs were bipedal, the great sauropods supported their thirty- or forty-ton bodies on four stout, pillarlike legs. They had long, thick tails and enormous necks topped by ridiculously tiny heads.

The fossil bones of these giants among the giants were first unearthed in quantity by Cope and Marsh. By the early years of this century, restored skeletons (some nearly ninety feet long) could be found in leading museums in the United States and Europe. These skeletons immediately became the objects of the greatest fascination for the general public. Even today, a good sauropod skeleton will be the centerpiece of most museum dinosaur exhibits.

When O. C. Marsh first reconstructed *Brontosaurus* in 1883, he had the creature standing well above the ground, supported by straight legs. That's the way an elephant stands, but it's not the way a lizard stands—a fact pointed out by a few brave scientists. However, Marsh's influence was great, and most of the museum reconstructions followed the pattern he set.

Still the critics objected. If *Brontosaurus* and its

Museum employees prepare the skeleton of a giant sauropod for exhibition.

kin were reptiles, they said, why weren't they shown standing like reptiles? Their legs should sprawl like those of an alligator or a lizard!

Eventually, paleontologists at the American Museum of Natural History tried to reconstruct a *Brontosaurus* skeleton along strictly reptilian lines. It just didn't work. Other attempts to make the sauropods more lizardlike resulted in grotesque and unlikely monstrosities. In one case, a "lizardlike" *Diplodocus* would not have been able to move without scraping a deep rut in the ground with its belly.

The most impressive thing about the great sauropods are their sheer bulk. But that also presents problems for the reptile–dinosaur identification. How could a low-energy reptile support a body of that size and a neck of that length without simply falling over in exhaustion? And once it fell over, how would it ever get up again? A solution of sorts was to assume that the great sauropods were basically swamp dwellers who spent all or most of their time up to their very long necks in water. The water would support their bulk. The sauropods' way of life would resemble that of the modern hippopotamus. (The hippo can and does leave the water, but it is most at home there.)

For about seventy years, the image of the sauropods as semiaquatic giants too large and clumsy to support their own weight out of the water was the dominant one. Now, this image has been strongly challenged by those who believe the dinosaurs were warm-blooded.

If the dinosaurs were endothermic, says Robert T. Bakker, the colossal sauropods didn't need to spend their lives wallowing in the water. They could have walked, firmly and swiftly, on the land, their tails held out stiffly behind them so as not to slow their progress, and their heads held high in the air. They could have browsed on the tops of the tall pines and cycads that grew in profusion during their time. They would have resembled something like a cross between a giraffe and an elephant, though they were far, far larger than either.

The sauropods evidently traveled in herds. Paleontologists have found footprints that indicate that a large number of these creatures were traveling together in one direction.

Bakker suggests that the impact of these giants would have changed the face of the land over which they passed. Not only would they have stripped the taller trees and plants, but they would have trampled the undergrowth beneath their enormous feet. "Smaller herbivorous dinosaurs adapted to open woodlands and plains must have depended on sauropods for keeping such habitats from being overrun by thick jungle," Bakker wrote in 1971.

The sauropods had no armor or horns or other external protection. Sheer size would have made adults invulnerable to attack by all but the largest and hungriest of predators. And an adult sauropod must have been able to swing its enormous tail with deadly force, or rear up on its hind legs and flail away with its front legs. The young, however, would have been in constant danger unless they had some form of protection. Bakker has suggested that the herd provided such protection. One reason that mammals of today (for example, elephants) form herds is to protect their young. If the sauropods did this, it is yet another indication that they might have been warm-blooded.

Adrian Desmond has written, "The sight of . . . great herds of sauropods moving through the Jurassic forests, with young the size of fully grown elephants protected by a ring of weathered old bulls, must have been one of the most awe-inspiring of any period during Earth history."

Awe-inspiring, perhaps—but would it have been possible? Here is where we begin to see problems with the idea of sauropods as warm-blooded creatures.

The sauropods had impossibly small brains for their size. Was there enough intelligence there for them to sustain a herding way of life? It doesn't take a lot of brains to play follow-the-leader, but it takes some.

More pressing is the problem of food. Even if we assume that the sauropods were slow-moving, low-energy reptiles, it's hard to imagine how they could have gotten enough to eat. They had tiny heads and weak teeth. Could they have forced enough food through their small mouths to support their huge bodies? Could they have done so day after day without destroying their weak teeth?

As I said earlier, endothermic animals need up to ten times as much food as ectothermic ones. So, if we assume the sauropods were warm-blooded, they would have had to eat that much more—perhaps as much as half a ton of vegetable matter each and every day! Granted, the warm-blooded sauropod would be more active in searching out food—it would spend more time eating and less time sleeping. Still, it does not seem possible that a warm-blooded sauropod could have gotten enough to eat, even if it *never* slept. And how about chewing that much food, nipping off buds, fruit, and twigs, as browsing animals normally do? Wouldn't that have utterly destroyed even large, strong teeth, and don't sauropod teeth look ridiculously inadequate for such a task? As I've just said, the teeth look too weak even for a reptilian sauropod! Nevertheless, the sauropods existed in great numbers. Whether cold- or warm-blooded, they somehow managed to get enough to eat.

Mysteries remain, and probably always will. Dr. Eugene S. Gaffney of the American Museum of Natural History says, "You have to face the fact that many questions about the dinosaurs are simply not resolvable, and [I think] that includes the question of warm-bloodedness."

Paleontology is an interesting field partly because there *are* so many mysteries in it. No matter how many fossil clues we may find, there are a few more waiting to be sought out—a few pieces of the puzzle are always missing. This is true not only of dinosaurs, but also of other creatures that lived when the dinosaurs did. Let's look at the intriguing mystery of the gigantic pterosaurs.

Pterosaurs were flying creatures that dominated the skies during the age of dinosaurs. Their existence

Pterosaur, the flying creature that dominated the skies during the age of the dinosaurs.

has been known for a long time, relatively speaking. Their fossils were first discovered at the end of the eighteenth century, decades before the dinosaurs were known. The fossil creatures were obviously very unlike any living thing. In fact, pterosaur fossils were among the first fossils to make people realize that the life on this Earth had, at one time, looked very different.

Pterosaur fossils have been found on every continent except Antarctica. A large number of different species of pterosaur existed over a long period of time. The pterosaurs all died out at about the same time as the dinosaurs.

The first fossil pterosaurs to be discovered were fairly small, about the size of a modern sparrow. But as time went on, larger and larger specimens were found, until Cope and Marsh each independently discovered the remains of pterosaurs that may have had wingspreads of over twenty feet. These huge pterosaurs were given the name *Pteranodon*, which means "winged and toothless." *Pteranodon* was a really bizarre-looking creature with a long toothless beak, a huge bony crest on the back of its skull, enormous wings, and a relatively tiny body.

Since the discovery of these "giants of the air," scientists have been fascinated by them, for *Pteranodon* was a marvel of aeronautical engineering. In order to get off the ground at all, *Pteranodon* had to be extremely light. Estimates are that it weighed less than forty pounds, and perhaps as little as twenty. Most of the weight saving came in the bones, which were hollow. (Birds have hollow bones too, but many engineers have said that pterosaurs were more efficiently constructed than birds.)

It is generally accepted that the larger pterosaurs were more gliders than fliers, for they simply didn't have the muscles to constantly flap their enormous wings. They must have gotten most of their lift from air currents that they caught with their outsized wings.

There are many puzzles about pterosaurs, particularly about large ones like *Pteranodon*. How did they become airborne? How were they able to land without breaking their fragile bones and tearing their paper-thin wings? How exactly did they catch their food? To this day, scientists argue about the answers to these and other questions. But for many years, there was one thing that practically everyone agreed upon. It was this: Not only was *Pteranodon* the largest flying creature that had ever lived, it was the largest flying creature that ever *could* have lived. (The fragmentary remains of a vulture that may have been nearly as large were found recently in Argentina.)

The larger a flying animal becomes, the more powerful it must be, and, therefore, the more muscles it needs. But the muscles make it heavier still, and there comes a point at which the creature becomes too large and too heavy to sustain its own weight. According to most calculations, *Pteranodon* had just about reached that limit.

Then, in 1972, all previous calculations had to be thrown away, because Douglas A. Lawson, then a student at the University of Texas, discovered fragmentary remains from an unknown species of pterosaur in the Big Bend National Park in West Texas. To date, no complete skeleton of this creature has been found. But the bones that have been found are of an unprecedented size, and indicate that this marvel of the air had a wingspread of up to fifty feet—making it twice as large as *Pteranodon*. The new pterosaur has been given the name *Quetzalcoatlus*, after the Toltec and Aztec god who took the form of a feathered serpent.

If there are many mysteries about *Pteranodon* and the smaller pterosaurs, there are even more surrounding *Quetzalcoatlus*, the "impossible animal." The most obvious question is, how was it able to fly at all? Until more extensive remains are found, we can only take wild guesses at the answers to such questions. The only thing it is safe to say is that it is *not* safe to predict that anything is impossible when it comes to animals from the age of dinosaurs.

And, oh yes, the pterosaurs have been involved in the warm-blooded–cold-blooded controversy. Those who believe that the dinosaurs were endothermic insist that the pterosaurs had to be endothermic, too. As evidence, they cite the 1971 discovery by a Russian zoologist of a small fossil pterosaur that was covered with hair. Only warm-blooded creatures have, or need, coverings like hair or feathers. Some paleontologists have suggested that large pterosaurs like *Pteranodon* were covered with a coat of white fur. Such a coat would have reflected the sun and thus would have kept the pterosaur from overheating.

With all of these new discoveries and theories, our

picture of the world of the dinosaurs has become stranger than ever. It is a world in which ten-ton horned dinosaurs gallop along at thirty miles an hour, pursued by giant carnivores that can run or possibly jump along at an even greater speed. It is a world in which herds of thirty-ton brontosaurs—heads high, tails held out stiffly behind them—cut broad swaths through the jungle, gobbling up or trampling down everything in sight in their never-ending search for enough food. And through the skies of this world soar white, furry pterosaurs with wingspans of fifty feet. . . .

The world of the dinosaurs, it seems, was far different and far stranger than we imagined just a few years ago!

CHAPTER 4

What Killed
the Dinosaurs?

There are two things everybody knows about dinosaurs. The first is that they were big, and the second is that they are extinct. As I said in the last chapter, not *all* dinosaurs were big. And in the next chapter, I'll present a small quibble with the proposition that dinosaurs are extinct. But, for the moment, let us adopt the majority view that they *are* extinct, defunct, completely gone.

Because the dinosaurs are extinct, most people have the idea that they were somehow "failures." But, as I have already pointed out, dinosaurs were anything but failures. The dinosaurs may have been fast and reasonably intelligent. They were unquestionably the absolute masters of the Earth's land surface for some 140 million years. Yet the question arises: If they were so successful, why did they die out? It's a good question, for which there are no good answers. Indeed, the death of the dinosaurs is the single greatest mystery in paleontology, and one of the most compelling mysteries in all of science. Its fascination reaches well beyond the scientific community.

At one time, there was a sort of general assumption that the dinosaurs became extinct because they'd been around too long and had gotten "old." People (including many scientists) thought that species, like individuals, went through regular life cycles in which they matured, grew old, and then died. We now know that species are not like individuals, and do not have a predetermined "life expectancy." Turtles and crocodiles have been around ever since the time of the dinosaurs, and they show no signs of dying out. Horseshoe crabs and limpets have been around a lot longer, and they are still doing very nicely, thank you.

Another general assumption was that dinosaurs somehow got too big and too overspecialized, and then, when they failed to "adapt," they died off. This is the view of the dinosaur as something obsolete. But questions arise. Too big for what? Too overspecialized for what? Failed to adapt to what?

We have to remember that there were many different species of dinosaur. Some were large, others not so large. Some were grotesquely horned and armored, others were sleek and streamlined in appearance. Some may have been very specialized in their habits, but others surely were not. Over the 140 million years of dinosaurian dominance, many species of dinosaur died off and were replaced by others. *Stegosaurus*, with its strangely armored back and walnut-sized brain, died out well before other dinosaurs did. But the duckbilled dinosaurs, many of which supported fantastically elaborate crests, were

This Charles R. Knight mural shows the type of dinosaurs that existed near the end of the Cretaceous period, shortly before the dinosaurs disappeared.

flourishing to the last. Toward the end of the age of dinosaurs the great sauropods, like *Brontosaurus*, had been reduced in numbers, but *Tyrannosaurus*, with its saberlike teeth, was still there. Extinction of some species and their replacement by others has been a common and constant occurrence in Earth history. But what happened to the dinosaurs some sixty-five million years ago, at the end of the geologic pe-

riod called the Cretaceous, was not at all common. At that time *all* the dinosaurs died out, and they were not replaced. That is *not* an ordinary event in Earth history.

There is some dispute over how quickly the extinction of the dinosaurs took place. Some scientists believe that the total number of dinosaur species had become smaller toward the end of the Cretaceous. This would indicate that the dinosaurs were already in decline before the end finally came. Other scientists claim that this "decline" is really an illusion, and that dinosaurs were as numerous and dominant as ever right up to the very end.

Dinosaur fossils can be dated only in a very broad and general way, so there is no way of telling whether the dinosaurs became extinct overnight, or over a period of a million years. But given the many millions of years of Earth's geologic history, one million years *is* almost overnight. And everyone agrees that whether it took place over a day or a million years, the extinction of all the species of dinosaurs seems freakishly abrupt.

For a long time, there was a general impression that major climatic changes at the end of the Cretaceous were responsible for the death of the dinosaurs. The Cretaceous world was pictured as warm, flat, swampy, and overgrown with soft vegetation. The post-Cretaceous world was cooler; there were mountains and highlands, and many of the swamps had dried up. Vegetation was more modern, with an abundance of grasses and other hard-to-chew plants. The dinosaurs, already "too big" and "too overspecialized," were supposedly unable to adapt to these changes in their environment.

Some major changes did indeed take place at the end of the Cretaceous. But Earth is not a dead planet—major changes are *always* taking place. The pace of change may be slow, but the fact of change is undeniable. Now, by the end of the Cretaceous, the dinosaurs had been on Earth for 140 million years. During that long period, the world had changed radically several times. Still the dinosaurs had adapted and flourished. As old species died out, new ones took their places in the new world. As far as we can determine, the geologic and climatic changes that occurred at the end of the Cretaceous were no greater than those the dinosaurs had seen before. Some dinosaurs might have suffered because of those changes, but in the normal course of events others should have survived, just as they had for so many millions of years. Yet they didn't.

If the dinosaurs were warm-blooded, as now seems quite possible, they should have been even more capable of adapting to changing climates. Even if they were cold-blooded reptiles, many of them should have adapted successfully. As I just mentioned, reptiles like turtles and crocodiles were alive in the time of the dinosaurs, and they are still alive today. Why would dinosaurs have been more vulnerable than these "ordinary" reptiles?

The geologic record shows no alteration at the end of the Cretaceous radical or abrupt enough to account for what happened.

Yet another general impression is that the dinosaurs were somehow bested in an evolutionary struggle with the mammals, and that *that* is why they died out. The idea is that Late Cretaceous mammals, while small, were faster, smarter, and in all ways superior to the slow-moving, slow-witted, and overbuilt dinosaurs. This view is appealing because it seems to imply progress. It is also appealing because it reflects well on us, since we are mammals and it is our ancestors that "won." But this theory has nothing but mammalian chauvinism to recommend it. We can no longer claim with any certainty that the early mammals were faster, more agile, or brainier than the dinosaurs. They may not even have taken better care of their young.

There is another, more compelling reason for casting the "mammalian superiority" theory into the dustbin of history. Mammals did not evolve after dinosaurs. Both mammals and dinosaurs appeared on the scene at about the same time, some two hundred million years ago, during the period of Earth history known as the Triassic. The ancestors of the mammals were a group of reptilelike creatures known as therapsids. The dinosaurs' ancestors were another group of reptilelike animals called thecodonts. The early dinosaurs and the early mammals started out with an equal chance to become the dominant group. In the competition for dominance of the Earth that took place over the next few million years, the dinosaurs were the clear and overwhelming victors. While the dinosaurs evolved into ever larger and more fantastic shapes, and controlled more and more of the Earth's ecological niches, mammals remained small and numerically insignificant. Most of these early mammals were about rat size and had to content themselves with eating seeds and insects. They must have spent no small amount of time trying to keep from being crushed beneath the feet of the giant dinosaurs. They would have been relatively safe from the larger carnivorous dinosaurs, which would have found them far too small to make a meal—too small perhaps even to notice. But the smaller carnivorous dinosaurs probably did feast on early mammals, for they almost certainly were as fast, agile, and intelligent as the mammals. And they were superbly adapted to catching and killing prey. While some mammals may have stolen dinosaur eggs, there was not a single early mammal that would have been capable of successfully attacking a full-grown dinosaur.

Yes, in the evolutionary struggle between dinosaurs and mammals, the dinosaurs were the clear winners. Mammals began to flourish only in the post-Cretaceous world, after the dinosaurs were safely gone. Today, mammals have become the dominant life form on the land. They have evolved to fill many of the ecological niches once filled by dinosaurs (though land mammals have never reached the spectacular size once attained by some dinosaurs). Quite possibly, this never would have happened if the dinosaurs had lived on. . . . Which brings us right back to the question of what happened to them.

At one time, great worldwide catastrophes were a popular way of explaining extinctions. Some considered fossils the remains of animals drowned in the flood of Noah. When it became clear that extinctions had taken place at different and widely separated periods of Earth history, a series of successive worldwide catastrophes was postulated. But as the science of geology began to develop in the nineteenth century, catastrophes began to lose favor as explanations for extinctions or major geologic changes.

Geologists were able to show that most major Earth changes—the uplifting of mountains, the movement of glaciers, the erosion of highlands, and so on—were part of a slow and gradual process. The Earth was far, far older than anyone had imagined. And, as more fossils were discovered and dated, it became clear that the extinction of some species and the appearance of others was also a slow and continuous process.

But the case of the extinction of the dinosaurs stood out in sharp contrast to the theories of gradual change. The dinosaurs—all of them, not just some—had died out very suddenly. This was an oddity, and no one quite knew what to do about it. So the puzzle just hung there while scientists hoped and assumed that some sort of evidence would turn up that would allow the extinction of dinosaurs to be fitted in with the rest of Earth history.

Unfortunately, the wrong sort of evidence kept turning up. Not only had the dinosaurs died out at the end of the Cretaceous—so had all the pterosaurs and great marine reptiles. No large animal of *any* kind survived the end of the Cretaceous. Small, primitive mammals lived on; so did small ancestors of modern turtles, lizards, and birds. But all the big animals disappeared. For the first few million years after the end of the Cretaceous, the Earth was strangely empty of large-sized life. It was like an abandoned city inhabited only by rats and cockroaches. Slowly larger animals began to evolve, but the new land creatures never reached the size of the larger dinosaurs.

Weirder still, it wasn't just the large animals that died at the end of the Cretaceous. The fossil record indicates that many species of plankton and marine mollusks also became extinct. The more scientists discovered, the deeper and more ominous the puzzle of these extinctions became. We were no longer dealing with the death of a species or a group of species, or even with the death of an entire class of animals like the dinosaurs. This was mass death, involving hundreds of different species from all parts of the animal kingdom. (There is also evidence of a major change in plant life, though the case here is not so clear.) Something extraordinary, overwhelming, and possibly terrifying had happened at the end of the Cretaceous. Suddenly catastrophies were back in favor. They have always had a good deal of popular appeal anyway, and now science had no choice but to take them seriously again.

The extinctions could not have been caused by a worldwide flood, mass volcanic explosions and earthquakes, or a sudden ice age. Any of these cataclysmic events would have left unmistakable evidence in the geologic record. As I have said, there is no evidence in the geologic record that anything very unusual happened at the end of the Cretaceous—except, of course, that so many things, from gigantic dinosaurs to tiny plankton, suddenly died out!

Scientists began to look beyond the Earth to find the explanation for this "great death." One theory that has enjoyed considerable popularity in recent years is that the extinctions were brought about by the sudden explosion of a nearby star.

Normally stars go through a relatively stable life cycle from their birth to their death. But sometimes, for reasons we can only guess at, a star will explode suddenly and violently. It becomes a supernova. It is quite beyond our powers to adequately explain or even imagine the enormity of such an explosion.

In the year 1054, Chinese astronomers (who kept the most careful and certainly the longest record of astronomical events) observed the sudden flaring of a new star in the sky. Its brightness faded after a short time and it disappeared from view, but modern astronomers with their telescopes have been able to find the remains of that "new star." It is what is now called the Crab Nebula, a diffuse mass of ionized gas—the remains of a star. What the Chinese had observed was a supernova, a star blowing itself apart.

When a star explodes, the area surrounding it is showered with radiation. The supernova that became the Crab Nebula was too far away to have any direct effect upon Earth, but a closer supernova could saturate the Earth with lethal doses of radiation. "Closer" is, of course, a relative term. In this case, it means a supernova within a few hundred light-years of our planet.

Could such a supernova have accounted for the extinction of the dinosaurs? Yes—but. When we're dealing with this sort of speculative material there is always a but, and sometimes there are several of them.

Certainly the dinosaurs would have been profoundly, even disastrously affected by any substantial increase in radiation, whether it came from a supernova or some other source. Being large land dwellers, they would have received a full dose of any radiation bombarding the Earth's surface. If the dose was high enough, they would have expired immediately from radiation damage to their cells. Lower doses of radiation could have caused cancer, sterility, or genetic changes, that would lead to the death of future generations. Pterosaurs would have been similarly affected, for they, too, were surface-dwelling animals, and some of them were quite large. On the other hand, primitive mammals must have spent part of their time in underground burrows, so they would have been protected from the worst effects of the radiation.

So far, so good. Radiation would zap dinosaurs and pterosaurs, but would not affect small mammals so profoundly. Dinosaurs and pterosaurs died out; small, primitive mammals did not. Up to this point, the supernova theory looks plausible.

However, water would also shield living things from the effects of direct radiation. Yet the great marine reptiles died out, and, more significantly, so did many types of plankton. The plankton, as tiny, simple organisms, should have been the least vulnerable to direct radiation.

There is also a good deal of scientific debate over how much hard radiation would have reached the Earth over what period of time. Today many scientists think that by the time the radiation from a supernova got here, it would be too diffuse to kill anything outright, even large, vulnerable animals. While it certainly cannot be ruled out, direct cosmic bombardment by radiation is now thought to be an unlikely cause for the extinction of the dinosaurs.

However, the radiation would not have had to kill the dinosaurs directly. A relatively minor increase in radiation would still have had major effects on the climate. One possible result would be a sudden, sharp cold spell. In this case, plant life would be decimated— the food supply of the herbivorous dinosaurs would be destroyed. Once the plant-eating dinosaurs were gone, the giant predators would soon follow. If the temperature increased after a few years, the plants might recover, but by then the dinosaurs would be gone.

In a world suddenly grown cold, the dinosaurs' great size would become a disadvantage. Under cold conditions, smaller reptiles would become sluggish, and when they got cold enough they would hibernate. Some might freeze to death, but others would survive. The dinosaurs, however, could not hibernate. This would be true whether they were cold-blooded reptiles (like lizards) or warm-blooded (like bears). For one thing, they were too big to crawl under logs or to find other shelter where they could hibernate. And then, they were adapted to living in a warm climate—cold snaps had just never been a problem for them. Like the elephant and the rhinoceros of today, they had no thick fur coats, because they had never needed them. And they weren't adapted to hibernate, because they'd never needed to. As Adrian Desmond put it, "Lizards had to be prepared to hibernate, but small changes in ambient temperature were easily combatted by the bulky dinosaurs. . . ." *Small* changes. But we're talking about a big change here. A big drop in temperature could have frozen all the dinosaurs that didn't starve to death first.

The temperature of the seas might also have dropped, and it would not have had to drop very far to kill off the huge marine reptiles and the tiny plankton, both of which would have been sensitive to changes in temperature.

Scientists have searched long and hard for some evidence that a star exploded near Earth at the end of the Cretaceous. So far, they have found none. The supernova theory got a lot of attention when it was first proposed, but today, for lack of supporting evidence, it remains just that—a theory.

There are more exotic theories to explain the mass extinctions at the end of the Cretaceous. Perhaps the most exotic holds that the Earth was struck by a rice-sized fragment from a black hole. This fragment went in one side of the Earth and came out the other, and in so doing thoroughly disrupted the weather patterns of the planet.

A black hole is what remains of a giant star that has collapsed in upon itself; it is incredibly dense. In theory, at least, a tiny particle from a black hole could pass right through the Earth and come out the other side. But whether this actually happened—indeed, whether such things as black holes really exist at all—is not known. The theory was proposed at a time when there was a good deal of talk about black holes. The idea got a lot of publicity because it was so bizarre, but it never picked up much support in the scientific community.

Another catastrophe-from-space theory has become popular quite recently. This one holds that at the end of the Cretaceous the Earth collided with a gigantic meteorite, one that was about six miles in diameter. A body that big should more properly be called an asteroid. Asteroids of about that size have passed close to the Earth fairly often, and a collision is not impossible.

The collision that supposedly took place sixty-five million years ago would have profoundly altered the climate of the Earth. For one thing, huge clouds of dust would have been thrown up. These would have blocked most of the sunlight coming to Earth for three or four years. "Turning off the light" in this way would not only have lowered the world's temperature, it would have disrupted the growth of plants. I've already explained how lower temperature and the death of plants would affect the dinosaurs. Add a lack of sunlight and you've got a formula for the quick death of many kinds of creatures.

One of the chief proponents of the asteroid theory is Dr. Walter Alvarez of the Lawrence–Berkeley Laboratory in California. He believes that he has found traces of the dust in sedimentary rocks that mark the boundary layer between Cretaceous and post-Cretaceous rocks. Meanwhile, some scientists who back this theory say that the asteroid struck in an area now covered by water and that that is why a crater is not visible. (Indeed, some think that part of the Pacific Ocean is an impact crater.)

There are just about as many theories to account for the extinction of the dinosaurs as there are people to construct them. All of this theorizing is being done at the very outer edges of scientific knowledge. The evidence we must deal with is fragmentary and difficult to interpret. The dinosaurs vanished so very long ago. And we are not used to dealing with catastrophes of a magnitude that would explain the decimation of the Cretaceous world. We can only guess at what might happen if a supernova exploded nearby, or if the Earth was struck by a piece of a black hole or a six-mile-wide asteroid. In a way, it is fortunate that we have no direct experience to guide us. If we had, we probably wouldn't be here.

In such situations speculation can and usually does run wild, for there is little chance that anyone's theory will be proved definitely wrong. We're talking here about one of those puzzles for which we may never really find a solution. But it's fun to speculate about what happened. Well, perhaps not *entirely* fun . . . if you begin to think that there was a catastrophe at the end of the Cretaceous that wiped out the dinosaurs, you may begin to wonder if there will be another one in the future that will do the same to the human race. That's an unsettling thought. Let's get back to the dinosaurs, and think how different the world might look today if whatever happened had *not* happened. Perhaps mammals would not have become the dominant life form. Possibly dinosaurian evolution would have continued, and the dinosaurs would have developed more efficient bodies and larger brains. Today tiny mammals might still be skittering around at the feet of dinosaurian overlords. And it might have been dinosaurs that landed on the moon.

We will never know whether dinosaurs would have evolved toward greater intelligence, because the dinosaurs have no descendants. Or do they?

It was once believed that the dinosaurs simply had no descendants in the modern world. Now many scientists believe otherwise. They think that modern birds may be descended from the dinosaurs. Those starlings in your yard may have a *Tyrannosaurus* in their family tree. Treat them with more respect.

Actually, there is nothing particularly new in the idea that there is a close relationship between birds and dinosaurs. The many anatomical similarities have been pointed out repeatedly for more than a century. The first dinosaur footprints ever found were initially identified as the footprints of giant birds. But somehow, the idea of a close relationship between dinosaurs and birds has been hard to take seriously.

One of the most startling fossil finds of all time was made in Bavaria in 1861. Workmen in a quarry found the exceptionally detailed and well-preserved fossil of a small creature that looked to be half reptile and half bird. The little animal had a tail and claws like a reptile, but the limestone in which it was embedded also contained a clear imprint of wings and feathers. The creature was given the name *Archaeopteryx*, or "ancient feather," for it came from rocks that were perhaps 150 million years old. In 1861, *Archaeopteryx* was older than any known dinosaur.

Since that time, other specimens of *Archaeopteryx* have been found, and there has been continuing controversy over just how to classify the creature. In recent years, supporters of the concept of the warm-blooded dinosaur have advanced a new answer for the old question. They say that *Archaeopteryx* is not "the first bird," as has often been claimed, but rather is a small feathered dinosaur of a type that later evolved into true birds. Moreover, they say that birds should be considered a subclass of dinosaurs, instead of a class by themselves. Their argument goes like this: While the many anatomical similarities between birds and dinosaurs have long been known, the feathers of *Archaeopteryx* always presented a problem. Feathers (like hair) are a covering used to retain body

Archaeopteryx: either the first bird or a small, feathered dinosaur—or something in between. The creature, about the size of a crow, was probably not capable of true flight. It may have used its wings for gliding, or simply to trap food.

heat. As long as the dinosaurs were assumed to be cold-blooded, they didn't "need" feathers. But if the dinosaurs were warm-blooded, they certainly might have needed a covering like feathers. In other words, *Archaeopteryx* would not have to have been a true bird to have feathers. (Indeed, hints of feathers have been found in the fossils of some other dinosaurs such as *Compsognathus*.)

A bird's feathers are also necessary in flying, but it is highly unlikely that *Archaeopteryx* was able to fly. Though its arms had been modified into wings, it lacked the powerful muscles needed for true flight. It may have been able to climb trees with its claws and then glide from branch to branch with the aid of its wings, much as flying squirrels do today. But it is more likely that *Archaeopteryx* was a ground dweller that used its feathered wings to trap the insects that formed the major part of its diet. The adaptation of the wings and feathers for flying would come later.

Birds, like mammals, remained a suppressed race during the Mesozoic, the 140-million-year period when dinosaurs ruled the land. Mesozoic birds were tiny, and the skies were dominated by the much larger pterosaurs, to which the birds were not related. Only after the mass deaths at the end of the Cretaceous did birds begin to prosper—and then not always in the air. Many post-Cretaceous birds were not fliers, but runners. Apparently they were trying to take over many of the ecological niches left open when the dinosaurs disappeared. There was even a giant of a bird, the seven-foot-tall *Diatryma*, living in what is now Wyoming in post-Cretaceous times. This creature had massive bones and an enormous beaked skull.

For several million years, large flightless birds

The ostrich and other large flightless birds resemble dinosaurs more closely than any other living creatures.

competed successfully with mammals for a dominant position on the land. But ultimately the mammals won out, and the flightless birds were reduced in numbers and range. Birds, however, have reigned supreme in the skies since post-Cretaceous times. The only flying mammal, the bat, is a successful animal, but it is really no competition for the birds.

The large flightless birds have not disappeared entirely from today's world. If you wish to see the living animals that most closely resemble the dinosaurs, I suggest that you go to the bird house at the zoo. Take a good look at today's large flightless birds—the ostrich, the emu, the cassowary. No creatures alive today are built more like our ancient friends, the dinosaurs.

CHAPTER 5

Dinosaurs Alive!

The fondest dream of all who have ever been fascinated by dinosaurs is that somewhere, somehow, there exists a real "lost world," a place where dinosaurs still survive. Imagination places this lost world in the midst of some steamy jungle, or on some remote volcanic island. In such a place there might be a "land that time forgot" where the dinosaurs of the primordial world live on.

That theme has been a common enough one in science fiction. Most of the really good lost-world type of science fiction was written back in the late nineteenth and early twentieth centuries. Today, writers generally displace their lost worlds to distant planets or entirely mythical worlds. But eighty or ninety years ago, large parts of the world's jungles could still be considered unexplored, or at least underexplored, and the world's islands were not fully charted. In those days, it seemed possible that a *real* "lost world" might exist on our own planet, tucked away in some remote corner.

But even a century ago the pioneer paleontologists did not think there were any living dinosaurs. All the fossils they found were tens of millions of years old. Yet for men like Cope and Marsh, the amount of fossil dinosaur material available was limited and fragmentary. So, ninety years ago, one could speculate that *perhaps* evidence of the survival of some dinosaurs had simply been overlooked. But today, after a century and a half of intensive fossil hunting throughout the entire world, we can say with confidence that there is no evidence that any dinosaur survived the Cretaceous period. The latest evidence that we have for dinosaurs is at least sixty million years old. There is not a single bone, or tooth, or footprint, or anything else to even hint that a single dinosaur has survived till the present day. Scientists agree that the dinosaurs are extinct—completely, utterly, totally. "The proof of the geologic record on this score is irrefutable," says paleontologist Edwin H. Colbert.

But did I hear someone say, "What about the coelacanth?" Every time one insists that the dinosaurs are extinct, there is someone around to bring up the coelacanth! So we had better tackle that argument right away.

The coelacanths were large fish with well-developed lower fins that looked rather like legs. Fish of this type flourished during the Mesozoic Era (the time of the dinosaurs), but they apparently died out even before the dinosaurs did. No trace of any coelacanth appeared in the fossil record until you got about seventy million years back, and so scientists quite confidently declared that the coelacanth was extinct. The EXTINCT label remained in place until December 22, 1938, when a coelacanth was caught by fishermen off the coast of South Africa.

The discovery of this present-day coelacanth created an enormous sensation throughout the world. Scientists offered a large reward for the capture of another of these singular creatures. Surely there had to be more than one surviving coelacanth. But for nearly fifteen years, it seemed that there wasn't. Finally, in 1952, another of the creatures was caught, this time north of the island of Madagascar. Since then, quite a number of other coelacanths have been caught. Their habits have been studied, and they have even been photographed alive and swimming in the water. It has turned out that the coelacanth, while not common, is not all that rare either. Fishermen of the Comoro Islands know it as *kombessa*. It is not often caught because it is a very wary creature and lives in places where fishermen rarely drop their nets.

It's often been said that if there are living coelacanths, there could be living dinosaurs, too. But there

are critical differences between the two kinds of creatures. Yes, the coelacanth is big (three to five feet
long, over one hundred pounds in weight). Its limb-
like fins, thick scales, bulging blue eyes, and very
toothy mouth make it noticeable. It can survive out of
water for several hours, and that, too, sets it apart
from the general run of fish. But, basically, the coelacanth is a large fish, and it looks like a large fish. To
the Comoro Islands fishermen (who, after all, are not
paleontologists), the *kombessa* is just another fish,
nothing to get particularly excited about. There are
larger and stranger-looking fish in the sea. But a dinosaur could not be overlooked so easily; it would never
pass as just another large jungle animal.

Then too, the coelacanth is a fish, a sea dweller. We
don't know nearly as much about the life in the sea as
we do about the life on land, and we knew a good deal
less about the sea in 1938 than we do today. So it is
not that difficult to see how we could have overlooked
a large sea creature like the coelacanth. But a dinosaur stomping around on the land (even in a remote
jungle) would be pretty hard to miss.

As I said before, I think we have to accept the idea
that there can be no such thing as a living dinosaur.
Still, the discovery of the coelacanth gives us hope,
however faint, that maybe a living dinosaur will be
found. And, clutching that hope firmly, we will now
explore some of the rumors concerning the possibility

that dinosaurs are alive today, or were in the quite recent past.

The best rumor for a very long time is also a very recent one. Tracing down rumors about living dinosaurs and other strange and unlikely creatures is the task of a small group of scientists who call themselves cryptozoologists. Cryptozoology, which concerns itself with such possibly mythical creatures as the Loch Ness monster and Bigfoot, is not a recognized branch of zoology. In fact, many scientists regard cryptozoology as a useless, even loony pursuit. Yet it undoubtedly has a romantic appeal—you want to believe that the cryptozoologists are going to discover that the "mythical" creatures are real. And they have come up with some extremely interesting cases, including the recent "African dinosaur."

The creature in question is supposed to live in the swampy jungles of the Congo and Zaire. It is known locally as *mokele-mbembe*. It is said to be about the size of an elephant, and supposedly is covered with smooth, brownish gray skin. It is also said to have a long, flexible neck, a very long and powerful tail, and huge clawed feet. According to the local Pygmies, these creatures spend much of their time in deep pools and subsurface caves in rivers and lakes. They emerge only to feed on fruits that grow at the waterside.

Stories of a dinosaurlike creature have been filter-

Cryptozoologists in Central Africa searching for a possible surviving dinosaur. Standing at the front of the canoe is Richard Greenwell of the International Society of Cryptozoology. Standing in the center of the canoe is Dr. Roy Mackal.

ing out of the swamp and jungle regions of Central Africa for many years. These stories and rumors have been rejected out of hand by most zoologists. But a couple of cryptozoologically inclined scientists, Dr.

Roy Mackal, of the University of Chicago, and James Powell, a Texas herpetologist, suspect that there might be something to the stories. Says Dr. Mackal, who also has a long-time interest in the Loch Ness monster, "We don't go around saying every myth is going to turn out to be a dragon, but we are willing to look."

Look they did. In February, 1980, they conducted a difficult and uncomfortable expedition to the remote and swampy Likouala River region of the Congo. While they didn't see *mokele-mbembe* themselves, they talked to many who said they had.

The best piece of evidence the two dinosaur hunters got was a report that one of the monsters had been killed in 1959 because it had disturbed fishermen on Lake Tele. The story went that the animal was killed with a spear and then cut up—a tedious job because of the creature's extremely long neck and tail. A rather fantastic end to the story was that everyone who ate meat from the creature died.

Mackal found that there appeared to be a superstitious dread attached to even talking about this type of creature, though many people did talk. Mackal and Powell have offered a two-thousand-dollar reward for any confirmed skeletal remains of *mokele-mbembe*. In 1981 Mackal went back to Africa. He didn't see the creature, or gather any physical evidence of its existence, but he did take photographs of what might have been its footprints.

Mackal and Powell acknowledge that the creatures, if they exist at all, must be extremely rare. By now they may well even be extinct. But the two men say they still have hopes of finding one alive. "We obtained eyewitness reports as recent as 1979. From the descriptions of the animal, we conclude that it is a species unknown to science as a living form."

One of these eyewitness reports is described in some detail by Mackal in an article called "Nessie's African Cousin." This article appeared in *Animal Kingdom*, an official publication of the New York Zoological Society. The witness was one Nicholas Mondongo; he came from a village on the fringes of the Likouala swamp region. He first described how his father had told of seeing the animal crawl out of the river and leave a track in the sand with its long tail. But Nicholas Mondongo did not just have to take his father's word for the existence of *mokele-mbembe*. One day while he was on a hunting trip along the Likouala aux Herbes River, he saw a *mokele-mbembe* "making the water run backwards" as it rose out of the river. Mackal continued the account:

It was early in the morning, probably around seven A.M. as far as we could determine, and the water in that part of the river was only three to six feet deep. He [Nicholas Mondongo] said that the reddish brown animal stood upright on its short legs, which he thought had been collapsed when it was submerged.

He saw its back and part of its tail. On the head was a frill resembling a chicken's comb. After about three minutes the animal submerged.

As to size, the witness estimated that the creature was about thirty-two feet long, ten feet of which were head and neck, the rest body and long, tapering tail. The head was somewhat larger in circumference than the neck.

It must be pointed out that in some details this description does not match other descriptions of *mokele-mbembe*, particularly in regard to the frill on the head. But, in general, the match is close enough. And it seems highly unlikely that this particular account was inspired by misidentification of a known animal.

The descriptions collected by Mackal and Powell led them to suspect that *mokele-mbembe* is a dinosaur, most probably one of the great sauropods. The long neck and tail plus the semiaquatic habits make the creature sound very much like *Brontosaurus*, as most scientists imagine (or once imagined) it to have been. Of course, *mokele-mbembe* would not be one of the real giants of the dinosaurian clan, for it is generally accounted to be merely elephant-sized, and the *Brontosaurus* of old was several times the size of any puny elephant. But dinosaurs have come in many sizes, and we can hardly expect that they would have remained unchanged over sixty-five million years or so. *Mokele-mbembe* may be a pygmy *Brontosaurus*.

Other scientists do not necessarily share Mackal's and Powell's enthusiasm for the *mokele-mbembe*. But some of them have begun to show an unaccustomed degree of respect for the idea that such a creature might exist. *Science 80*, a publication of the American Association for the Advancement of Science, stated, "Paleontologists like the Smithsonian's George Zug do not scoff at the efforts to document the existence of such 'cryptozoological' specimens. But they certainly withhold judgment until there is some direct physical evidence. . . ."

There is no "direct physical evidence" of a living dinosaur. But at least Mackal and Powell were very careful, thorough, and precise in collecting their stories about the *mokele-mbembe*. In the past, most of the stories of possible dinosaurs that came out of Africa were vague and confusing; often they came from sources of dubious reliability, or from known romancers. Usually such accounts have been classed simply as "travelers' tales," which means they are about as believable as "ghost stories" or "fairy tales." Still, the old stories might hint at something.

One of the earliest hints of a strange, dinosaurlike creature alive and well in the jungles of Africa came from the tales of Alfred Aloysius Horn, or "Trader" Horn, a late-Victorian traveler and adventurer. He wrote:

Aye, and behind the Cameroons there's things living we know nothing about. I could'a made books about many things. The Jago-Nini they say is still in the swamps and rivers. Giant diver it means. Comes out of the water and devours people. Old men'll tell you what their grandfathers saw, but they still believe it's there. Same as the Amali I've always taken it to be. I've seen the Amali's footprint. About the size of a good frying pan in circumference, and three claws instead o' five. There are some very big lakes behind the Cameroons. Used to be full of nice seal [manatees] at one time. Manga, they call it. But the Jago-Nini's wiped 'em out, the old natives say. . . .

What but some great creature like the Amali could account for the broken ivories we used to come across in the so-called elephant cemeteries? Fine old green ivory that's valuable for inlaying wood. Snapped right across in the thickest part and left in splinters. Aye! There's places in Africa where you get visions of primeval force.

Trader Horn's tales were immensely popular as entertainment, but people did not necessarily believe them, nor should they have. He was clearly reporting legends, and probably exaggerating what he heard at that—and yet perhaps there was something to this water-dwelling monster that he described. If it truly existed, it was certainly no known creature.

Horn's tale also points out a problem—the profusion and confusion of names. If one native speaks of the Jago-Nini and another of the Amali, is a single creature being talked of under two different local names? Or are two different large and possibly dinosaurlike creatures involved? It is difficult to tell. And of course the confusion grows as each new name is added to the list.

Another dinosaurlike creature from Central Africa is the *dingonek*. The best description we have of it comes from an early-twentieth-century writer on unknown creatures, C. W. Hobley. Hobley wrote that he at first considered stories about the *dingonek* to be typical travelers' tales.

> But I have since met a man who a few years back was wandering about the Mara River or Ngare Dubash, which rises in Sotik, crosses the Anglo-German boundary [between the African colonies held then by England and Germany], and runs into Lake Victoria in German territory. He emphatically asserts that he saw this beast. He was at the time about where the Mara River crosses the frontier, and the river was in high flood. The beast came floating down the river on a big log, and he estimated its length at about sixteen feet but would not be certain of the length, as its tail was in the water. He describes it as spotted like a leopard, covered with scales, and having a head like an otter; he did not see the long fangs described by Mr. Jordan [an American hunter who was supposed to have seen the beast somewhat earlier]. He fired at it

and hit it; it slid off the log into the water and was not seen again.

I made inquires of the District Commissioner, Kisii, Mr. Crampton, and he wrote recently and said he had visited the Amala River and made inquiries from the Masai in the neighborhood, and they knew of the beast, which they called Ol-umaina [one of several names for the *dingonek*], and described it as follows: about fifteen feet long, head like a dog, small ears marked somewhat after the fashion of a puff adder, has claws, short legs, short neck, is said to lie in the sun on the sand by the riverside and slip into the water when disturbed; when in the water only its head is visible.

Hobley, a pioneer cryptozoologist, was enthusiastic. He suggested that the thing might be a dinosaur, and added, "The [possible] survival of some race of saurians is a thing to thrill the imagination of the scientific world." Now, fifteen feet is not large for a dinosaur, but the existence of *any* previously unknown fifteen-foot creature in Central Africa would certainly "thrill the imagination of the scientific world." And not just the scientific world, either!

A more spectacular beast is the *chepekwe*, which was described by a number of early-twentieth-century travelers. One of them, Carl Hagenbeck, was a well-known animal collector. As is usual in such cases, Hagenbeck didn't see the creature himself. But:

Almost identical stories reached me, firstly, through one of my own travelers, and secondly, through an English gentleman who had been shooting big game in Central Africa. The reports were thus quite independent of each other. The natives, it seemed, had told both my informants that in the depths of the great swamps there dwelt a huge monster, half elephant, half dragon. This, however, is not the only evidence for the existence of the animal. It is now several decades ago since Menges [another animal collector who often worked for Hagenbeck]—who is, of course, perfectly reliable—heard a precisely similar story from the Negroes; and still more remarkable, on the walls of certain caverns in Central Africa there are to be found actual drawings of this strange creature. [Just what drawings Hagenbeck is referring to is unknown.] From what I have heard of the animal, it seems to me that it can only be some kind of dinosaur, seemingly akin to the *Brontosaurus*. As the stories come from so many different sources, and all tend to substantiate each other, I am almost convinced that some such reptile must be still in existence. At great expense, therefore, I sent out an expedition to find the monster, but unfortunately they were compelled to return without having proved anything, either one way or the other. In the part of Africa where the animal is said to exist, there are enormous swamps, hundreds of square miles in extent, and my travelers [suffered] very severe attacks of fever.

Another creature of dinosaurian proportions was

described by John G. Millais in his book about his travels in Africa:

The late King Lewanika, who was much interested in the study of the animals of his kingdom, Barotseland, frequently heard from his people of some great aquatic reptile, possessing a body larger than that of an elephant, which lived in the great swamps near his town. He therefore gave strict orders that the next time one was seen he should be told, and he would at once go himself and visit the place. In the following year three men rushed into his court house one day in a great state of excitement, and said they had just seen the monster lying on the edge of the marsh, and that on viewing them it had retreated on its belly, and slid into the deep water. The beast was said to be of colossal size, with legs like a gigantic lizard, and possessing a long neck. It was also said to be taller than a man, [with] a head like a snake.

Lewanika at once rode to the spot and saw a large space where the reeds had been flattened down, and a broad path, with water flowing into the recently disturbed mud, made to the water's edge. He described the channel made by the body of the supposed monster to Colonel Harding, the British Resident, as "as large as a full-sized wagon from which the wheels had been removed" [about four and a half feet wide].

In 1932, a Swiss zoologist named A. Monard went to Angola to try to trace down rumors of a huge reptilian monster called *libata*, which was supposed to be both very rare and very vicious. After considerable investigation, Dr. Monard came to the conclusion that the creature was really a large crocodile—crocodiles were quite common in the region. But he still thought dinosaurs might survive somewhere. He wrote:

> The existence of a large saurian descended from the reptiles of the Mesozoic Era is by no means theoretically impossible. Though every continent has been crossed and recrossed, most travelers follow much the same track, and there are still holes in the net to be explored. There have been several reports that some kind of "Brontosaurus" survives, and several expeditions have even gone to look for it; the fact that they failed may merely prove that this prehistoric beast is very rare, or that it lives in country as inaccessible as the great swamps still are.

None of the many explorers and naturalists who have gone off in search of the fabled Central African dinosaur claim to have actually seen it themselves. However, Ivan Sanderson, an eccentric British naturalist and writer, thought he *might* have gotten a glimpse of it in 1932. Years later when writing to his friend and fellow cryptozoologist Bernard Heuvelmans, Sanderson said that in 1932, while he was out exploring in the Congo region, he came across "vast hippolike tracks." The discovery was surprising, said Sanderson, for there were no hippos in the area. Supposedly they had all been driven out by a creature whose name Sanderson gave as *mbulu-e M'bembe.* A few months after finding the tracks, Sanderson had an even more astonishing experience.

Sanderson wrote how he and some companions were on the Upper Cross River. It was late in the day, and they had just entered a spot in the river called the Mamfe Pool:

> As we passed some all-but-submerged caves in the cliffside, we got the shock of our lives when the most terrific noises I have heard outside of warfare issued from one of the said caves and *something* (and it was the top of a head we both feel sure) much larger than a hippo rose out of the water for a moment, set up a large wave, and then gurgled under.

Anyone who knew Ivan Sanderson, as I did, will take this story with several grains of salt. In his travels, Sanderson always seemed able to encounter things that no one else did. Perhaps he was credulous, self-deceptive, a spinner of tall tales—or maybe he was just luckier than most. At any rate, if he did see the top of a dinosaur's head just above the surface of the water in that African pool, he was never able to bring back any tangible evidence of the creature's existence.

The account of a possible dinosaur that most impressed and influenced Dr. Roy Mackal was one made by Captain Freiherr von Stein zu Lausnitz. Von Stein was the leader of a German expedition to the Congo in 1913. He only heard about the creature:

> The animal is said to be brownish gray with a smooth skin, its size approximately that of an elephant, at least that of a hippopotamus. It is said to have a long and very flexible neck and only one tooth, but a very long one—some say it is a horn. A few spoke about a long muscular tail like that of an alligator. Canoes coming near it are said to be doomed; the animal is said to attack the vessels at once and kill the crews, but without eating the bodies. . . . It lives in the caves that have been washed out by the river in the clay of its shores at sharp bends. It is said to climb the shore even in the daytime in search of food; its diet is . . . entirely vegetable. The preferred plant was shown to me. It is a kind of liana with large white blossoms, a milky sap, and apple-like fruits. At the Ssombo River I was shown a path said to have been made by this animal in order to get at its food. The path was fresh and there were plants of the described type nearby.

Von Stein called the creature *mokele-mbembe*. He said it lived in the very region that Mackal and Powell later chose to investigate.

Dinosaurs were (or are) land animals. But, as we saw in Chapter 4, the giant land animals were not the only ones that disappeared at the end of the Cretaceous. The great marine reptiles and the pterosaurs also apparently died out then. Apparently. Might any of them have survived to the present day?

In the case of the sea creatures, particularly the plesiosaur, the evidence for survival is really quite good. At least, it is good when compared with the evidence for the survival of a dinosaur.

For years now, people have suspected that the elusive Loch Ness monster is a plesiosaur. Since 1933, when the modern era of Loch Ness monster sightings began, most of those who have reported getting a good look at the thing have said that it has a long neck and a small head—just like a plesiosaur. A motorcyclist named Donald Grant, who got the only reasonably good look at the monster when it was out of water, said that it had a long neck, a small head, a thick body, and a long, tapering tail—just like a plesiosaur.

One of the first—and certainly still the most famous—of all the Loch Ness monster photographs is the "London surgeon's" photo. Taken in April, 1934, it shows what appears to be a plesiosaurlike head and neck sticking up above the water.

Of course, the Loch Ness monster may not exist at all. If it does not exist, it certainly can't be a plesiosaur! However, recent attempts to photograph the monster have yielded some interesting results.

In 1972, an expedition sponsored by the Academy of Applied Science in New York went to Loch Ness in search of the monster. Using an underwater camera,

The famed "London surgeon's" photo of the Loch Ness monster showing what appears to be a plesiosaurlike head and neck.

the crew got two pictures of what appear to be the diamond-shaped flipper and part of the body of a large animal. The flipper was one that could, theoretically, belong to a plesiosaur.

In 1975, another AAS expedition obtained a number of dramatic underwater photos. One of these appears to show a small-headed, very long-necked creature swimming away from the camera. Yet another photo shows a rough, knobby object that some have called a close-up of the monster's face. No modern reconstructions of plesiosaurs envision the creatures as having faces of that sort. The plesiosaur's face is always shown as smooth and sleek. But, in truth, we do not really know what sort of face the prehistoric plesiosaur might have possessed. There is no absolute anatomical reason why the creature, or its modern descendant in Loch Ness, might not have a rough and knobby face.

After the 1975 photos were taken, it seemed only a matter of time and money before the Loch Ness monster mystery would be solved once and for all. If a small, underfinanced, and rather poorly equipped expedition like the AAS one could come up with such dramatic (though admittedly inconclusive) photos, then a well-equipped, well-staffed expedition would surely be able to deliver conclusive evidence that the monster existed, and the skeptics would be silenced for all times.

In 1976, the AAS, aided by *The New York Times*, sent out the most professionally staffed, best-equipped monster-hunting expedition Loch-Ness had ever seen. And what did all the experts with all their equipment have to show for a summer's work? Virtually nothing. They were unable to produce anything even vaguely comparable to the photos taken in 1972 and 1975. The 1976 expedition failed to find one bit of good evidence for the existence of the Loch Ness monster.

Since the failure of that extraordinarily well-publicized expedition, interest in the Loch Ness monster has slackened considerably. That, however, does not mean that people no longer "believe" in the Loch Ness monster. Many people still do believe in it—and most of them believe it is a plesiosaur.

Now we must ask one question. If the creature does exist, could it really be a plesiosaur or some close relative?

On one count, at least, the answer might seem to be "no." Plesiosaurs were sea-going creatures, and Loch Ness contains fresh water. But Loch Ness apparently once was an arm of the sea. In some long-past era, geologic changes cut the loch off from the sea, and over the ages the water has freshened. It is theoretically possible that sea creatures became isolated in the loch when it was cut off from the sea, and slowly adapted to the slowly changing condition of the water. And then, though the dolphin is a sea creature, there are some dolphins that live in fresh water. The reverse is also true. While the crocodile is basically a freshwater creature, there is a species of saltwater crocodile.

A major objection to the idea of monster-as-plesiosaur is this: Plesiosaurs were reptiles, and Loch Ness is too cold to support reptile life. The temperature of the water in the loch hovers in the neighborhood of forty-two degrees Fahrenheit all year long. If a cold-blooded reptile were to live in the loch, it would have to spend a great deal of time basking in the sun to raise its body temperature to a level at which it could function properly. However, Loch Ness is located quite far north, and at certain seasons of the year there is little if any sun for days on end. It's true that a reptilian Loch Ness monster might hibernate during the winter months, but in the warmer and sunnier months, it would have to spend most of its time lying in the sun. If nearly half a century of Loch Ness monster hunting has proved anything, it is that the monster rarely surfaces! Besides, scientific observation has pretty much proved that there are no large reptiles in northern latitudes.

Let's suppose for a moment that the plesiosaurs were not cold-blooded reptiles, but warm-blooded creatures. An endothermic plesiosaur would, in theory, be able to survive in the cold water of Loch Ness. The trouble with this supposition is that most scientists are firmly convinced that the plesiosaurs were reptiles. Here I think we have to score one against the idea of the monster-as-plesiosaur.

Next, it's necessary to make what may seem like an obvious point about the Loch Ness monster. It's this. Though the creature is almost always referred to in the singular, no one seriously believes that there is a single, immortal animal living in Loch Ness. Biologically speaking, the loch would have to contain a viable, breeding herd of the creatures. That could mean that there are as many as a hundred Loch Ness monsters! But if there are a hundred large monsters in the loch, why isn't one or another of them seen rather often? And what are they eating?

In modern times, there have been no reports that any Loch Ness monster has attacked anyone. So it's been assumed that the creatures are vegetarians. Yet the loch contains very little edible vegetable matter, and certainly not enough to sustain a whole population of large vegetarians. More likely, the creatures are fish eaters, as Dr. Roy Mackal has assumed. There *are* plenty of fish in the loch.

Plesiosaurs were fish eaters, and well adapted to catching their prey. If the Loch Ness monsters do eat fish, that's one more way in which they resemble the plesiosaurs of old.

Though the Loch Ness monster has gotten all the press, there are plenty of reports that other lakes in Scotland (and elsewhere) contain monsters. Generally the descriptions make these creatures sound like plesiosaurs. That may be because the creatures of Loch Morar and Lake Okanogan really are of the plesiosaur type . . . or it may simply be that all unknown lake creatures are assumed to look like the Loch Ness monster, which is assumed to look like a plesiosaur.

The sea monster or sea serpent has not received a great deal of public attention during the last few decades. Yet a century or so ago, the existence (or nonexistence) of large, strange, and unknown creatures in the sea was a hotly debated topic in scientific circles. Most scientists said the idea was nonsense. But a few insisted that a large and unknown creature, or perhaps several different kinds of large, unknown creatures, might well exist in the depths of the sea.

At one time, sea serpent sightings were reported regularly; this is no longer the case. That may be because fashions in monsters change, and people no longer make up sea monster stories. Or it may be because today's sailors are more sophisticated and have better equipment, and are not about to mistake a mass of floating seaweed or a whale for a sea monster. Or it may be because sea monsters will not surface in the vicinity of noisy powered vehicles. In the days of small, wooden-hulled sailing ships, the ship was a natural part of the sea environment. Perhaps sea monsters frequently surfaced near such vessels and were spotted by sailors. The same monsters might steer clear of the large, noisy ships of today.

While many sea monster sightings have pointed to the existence of a gigantic marine snake (hence the common term "sea serpent"), a number of stories also hint at the existence of a plesiosaurlike sea animal. In fact, the remains of plesiosaurs supposedly have been washed up on shores or plucked from the deep sea from time to time.

The badly rotted remains of what appeared to be a long-necked sea creature of unknown type were discovered on the beach at Stronsay in the Orkney Is-

lands in 1808. A somewhat similar-looking carcass
was washed ashore at Scituate, Massachusetts, in November 1970. And on April 10, 1977, a Japanese
fishing vessel off the coast of New Zealand pulled up
a long-necked carcass from a depth of one thousand
feet. Reports of this type have come from other
places over the years, too. In every case, what the
thing looks most like is the remains of a plesiosaur—
but remember that all of these stories concern badly
rotted remains.

In every one of the cases in which the remains have
been preserved long enough to be carefully studied,
they have turned out to be the remains of a shark,
usually the huge but harmless basking shark, which
may grow to a length of forty feet. How, you might
wonder, could anyone mistake a shark, no matter how
badly rotted, for a plesiosaur? The answer lies in
some peculiar features of shark anatomy.

The most obvious and memorable characteristic of
any shark are its huge, gaping jaws. The jaws of the
basking shark are enormous, though they are used
only to strain plankton, not to rip and tear flesh. Its
jaws are the anatomical feature that make a basking
shark look most like a shark. But the awesome jaws
are only loosely attached to the shark's cranium and
spinal column. When a basking shark dies and its
carcass begins to rot, the jaws are among the first
things to fall away. What remains at the front end of
the shark is a small cranium attached to a long spinal

"Sea monster" washed ashore at Scituate, Mass., in November 1970. The remains turned out to be those of a large shark.

column—giving the appearance of a creature with a long neck and a small head.

The next most prominent shark feature is the dorsal fin, but this is a fleshy appendage, and it, too, soon drops away from a rotting carcass. The shark's backbone extends into just one lobe of its two-lobed tail, and all evidence of the second lobe can simply rot away. If the bottom fins remain attached to the carcass, what is left is something that bears a remarkable resemblance to a plesiosaur: small head, long neck, thick body with four flippers, and a long, tapering tail. To further confuse the issue, the creature can even look as if it was once covered with short fur, for when a shark's muscle structure begins to rot, it may break up into individual whiskerlike fibers. Of course, plesiosaurs are not normally conceived of as hairy. Still, the "furry" look can definitely make shark remains seem lots less sharklike.

Now, if the remains are examined closely by an expert, they soon reveal their sharky origins. But at first glance, and in early news photos, it has often appeared that the survival of the plesiosaur into modern times has finally been proved.

All right, so we have been fooled a few times. That is no reason to adopt a totally skeptical attitude toward all sea monster reports. Some sightings may be genuine, and people may even have sighted a surviving plesiosaur from time to time, or at least a plesiosaurlike creature. The seas are wide and deep, and not nearly as well explored as the world's land areas. Each year they provide us with surprises, the discovery of forms of life that no one thought existed. Perhaps the discovery of a gigantic survivor from the age of the dinosaurs will be the ultimate surprise. That is really more of a hope than an expectation—but it is a heartfelt hope.

And finally, in the realm of sheer unfounded rumor,

there is the suggestion that some sort of surviving pterosaur has been found. From France in 1938 came a tale that a goose-sized pterosaur had been found alive inside a cave that had been sealed up for millions of years. The story went that the poor creature died shortly after being exposed to the air. Its remains were taken to a museum—but the report somehow neglected to say which museum, so there is no way of checking the tale.

Living pterosaurs have been reported in places as far away as West Africa and Java, but surely the most intriguing tales have come from the American West. Central to these stories is a creature from Native American mythology called the thunderbird.

The thunderbird was a bird of fabulous qualities and enormous size, according to the legends. Most anthropologists and folklorists who have studied the thunderbird legends believe that the creature was a sort of super eagle or super condor, and that all of its fabulous characteristics were simply exaggerations of the characteristics of real birds. But a few romantic eccentrics have always suspected that something more exotic was involved—that the basis of the thunderbird legends was actually a flying creature much larger than the eagle or the condor, a creature entirely unknown to modern science. The best piece of "evidence" for this belief is a photograph showing a "real" thunderbird. I put the word "evidence" in quotation marks for good and sufficient reasons. While a lot of people say that they have seen the remarkable photo, no one seems able to find a copy of it.

Back in 1886, out near Tombstone, Arizona, someone supposedly encountered a living thunderbird, killed it, and tacked it up, with its wings outstretched, on the side of a barn. In order to show the thing's size, six men stood in front of it with their arms spread wide, fingers touching, and they just about covered the creature's wingspan. From that, one can estimate that the thing had a wingspan of roughly forty feet.

Now, there is no known bird that has a forty-foot wingspread. As far as we know, the only thing that ever did have such a wingspread is the huge pterosaur *Quetzalcoatlus*, whose fossils were discovered in Texas in the 1970s. As we saw in Chapter 3, this creature may have had an even greater wingspread than the fabled thunderbird.

Some tales suggest that the creature shot in Arizona in 1886 did not really resemble a conventional bird, but rather was a featherless thing with a long head. That means it looked much as many think *Pteranodon* must have looked. Mind you, these stories were in circulation long before the gigantic *Quetzalcoatlus* was discovered. You'll recall that before the 1970s, people thought that a flying creature with a wingspread of much over twenty feet was a physical impossibility. So we can come to one of two conclusions. Either someone in Tombstone, Arizona, had an extremely vivid imagination, or someone actually did kill a "thunderbird" with a forty-foot wingspan.

If such a monster really was killed in 1886, isn't it likely that it was a huge surviving pterosaur? The photograph that was supposedly taken—of the creature tacked up on the barn, with the six men standing in front of it—might help us to answer this question. Hundreds of people say they have seen this particular thunderbird picture, but *no one* seems to have held on to a copy.

The picture supposedly was printed in the *Tombstone Epitaph*, the town's newspaper, but a check of the files of the paper dating back to 1884 revealed no trace of the photo. The editors of a popular magazine of weird and unusual happenings thought they might have printed the photo many years back, but a review of back issues revealed nothing. One leading cryptozoologist insisted that he had actually had a copy of the photo in his files, but that he had lent it out—he couldn't recall to whom—and it had never been returned. And so it goes. Chasing that particular photo has proved to be a deeply frustrating experience.

One must sadly draw the conclusion that the entire story of the Tombstone "thunderbird" is a fabrication, for without the photo itself, there is absolutely nothing to support the tale. We must look elsewhere than to the giant pterosaur for the origins of the thunderbird legends. I think we must also conclude that there are no pterosaurs alive today, and that none have been alive for millions of years. One can imagine a large prehistoric creature remaining undetected in the sea, or perhaps on land—but in the air? That requires a leap of faith I cannot make. It's amazing enough that such strange and unlikely creatures as the giant pterosaurs ever existed at all!

CHAPTER 6

The Literary Dinosaur

As soon as the existence of the dinosaurs became known, the huge creatures began to exert a fascination on writers, particularly writers of science fiction. It was Jules Verne, the acknowledged founding father of modern science fiction, who first used the dinosaur theme in a major work of fiction. Actually, he wrote of the great marine reptiles that lived during the age of the dinosaurs, for they were better known in his day.

Most of the early dinosaur stories told of modern men meeting with prehistoric creatures that had survived in some out-of-the-way place. Jules Verne set this trend. But Verne did not place his prehistoric creatures in an unexplored jungle or on a remote island; his primeval world was in the center of the hollow Earth.

His book was called *A Journey to the Centre of the Earth*, and it first appeared in Verne's native land, France, in 1864. It was the second of Verne's science-fiction novels. Before turning to science fiction, Verne had been an unhappy lawyer and an unsuccessful playwright. At the age of thirty-five, he tried his hand at writing a novel, and when *Five Weeks in a Balloon* came out, it was an immediate and enormous success. It was just the first of many; Verne eventually became one of the world's most widely read authors.

Some consider *A Journey to the Centre of the Earth* to be Verne's greatest novel. It is the chronicle of the adventures of the obsessed genius Professor Von Hardwigg, his nephew, and an Icelandic guide at the center of the hollow Earth. (The intrepid threesome get there by going down through an extinct volcano.)

Much of the Earth's interior, in this Verne tale, is covered by a vast Central Sea. While rafting across this great unknown ocean, the three adventurers spy two "monsters." One, according to Von Hardwigg, is "the world-renowned Ichthyosaurus or Great Fish Lizard." The other is "the Plesiosaurus . . . or Sea Crocodile."

Says the nephew/narrator:

At last have mortal eyes gazed upon two reptiles of the great primitive ocean! I see the flaming red eyes of the Ichthyosaurus, each as big as, or bigger than, a man's hand. Nature in its infinite wisdom has gifted this wondrous marine animal with an optical apparatus of extreme power, capable of resisting the pressure of the heavy layers of water which roll over him in the depth of the ocean where he usually feeds. It has by some authors truly been called the whale of the Saurian race, for it is as big and quick in its motions as our king of the seas. This one measures not less than a hundred feet in length, and I can form some idea of his girth when I see him lift his prodigious tail out of the waters. His jaw is of an awful size and strength, and, according to the best-informed naturalists, it does not contain less than a hundred and eighty-two teeth. . . .

The other was the mighty Plesiosaurus, a serpent with a cylindrical trunk, with a short, stumpy tail, with fins like a band of oars in a Roman galley.

Its whole body was covered by a carapace, or shell, and its neck, as flexible as that of a swan, rose more than thirty feet above the waves, a tower of animated flesh!

Verne's knowledge of what these creatures really looked like was rudimentary, and his descriptions were wrong. Oh, well—at least the monsters sound awesome.

Naturally, the two creatures are mortal enemies, and they immediately attack each other, thus setting the precedent for more than a century of "titanic

struggles" between various types of fictional dinosaurs or dinosaurlike creatures.

These animals attacked each other with inconceivable fury. Such a combat was never *seen* before by
mortal eyes, and to us, who did see it, it appeared more
like the phantasmagoric creation of a dream than anything else. They raised mountains of water, which
dashed in spray over the raft, already tossed to and
fro by the waves. Twenty times we seemed on the
point of being upset and hurled headlong into the
waves. Hideous hisses appeared to shake the gloomy
granite roof of that mighty cavern—hisses which carried terror to our hearts. The awful combatants held
each other in a tight embrace. I could not make out one
from the other. Still, the combat could not last for
ever; and woe unto us, whichsoever became the victor.

The eventual winner is the Ichthyosaurus:

Suddenly, at no great distance from us, an enormous mass rises out of the waters—the head of the
great Plesiosaurus. The terrible monster is now
wounded unto death. I can see nothing now of his
enormous body. All that can be distinguished is his
serpentlike neck, which he twists and curls in all the
agonies of death.

Illustration for the original edition of Jules Verne's *A Journey to the
Centre of the Earth*, showing the struggle between the Ichthyosaurus
and the Plesiosaurus.

After this, Ichthyosaurus disappears, allowing the three inner-earth explorers to go on to even more amazing adventures.

The illustration by E. Riou that accompanied this description of the battle of the sea monsters in the original edition of *A Journey to the Centre of the Earth* was obviously inspired by an illustration in Thomas Hawkins's 1840 volume *The Book of the Great Sea Dragons.* Thomas Hawkins (not to be confused with Waterhouse Hawkins, who built the Crystal Palace dinosaur reconstructions) was an eccentric amateur geologist and poet. His book on "sea dragons" was one of the first popular works on the newly discovered residents of the ancient Earth. The book was highly romantic and grandly inaccurate, yet it was also very influential. Engravings of prehistoric monsters locked in mortal combat illustrated the book; they were done by John Martin, and were among the first such illustrations ever attempted. The picture that inspired Riou showed an ichthyosaur battling a plesiosaur, and it's possible that Verne's whole scene was inspired by Hawkins's writing and Martin's engravings. At any rate, this episode in Verne's book inspired both later writers and the makers of horror films.

Today, Jules Verne enjoys a considerable reputation as a prophet of scientific discovery. He wrote about submarines and airships long before such things existed. However, *A Journey to the Centre of*

Illustration from Thomas Hawkins's *The Book of the Great Sea Dragons*, published in 1840, showing plesiosaurs, ichthyosaurs, and pterosaurs the way they were thought to have looked.

the Earth certainly did not predict future scientific discoveries. We have found no ichthyosaurs or plesiosaurs swimming about in a Central Sea in the center of the Earth, for the Earth is not hollow!

Of course, Verne's primary purpose was to produce an entertaining adventure story, not to predict the future. Still, he was a writer of *science* fiction, not fantasy. He strove for a degree of plausibility in all of his tales. Science-fiction writer Arthur Clarke says, "The strength of [Verne's] stories comes from the fact that even when his head was in the clouds, his feet were firmly on the ground."

How, then, did Jules Verne get the extraordinary idea that the Earth was hollow?

According to Arthur Clarke, Verne had met a scientist who had descended into the crater of the volcano on Stromboli, an island off the coast of Italy. (This island is in the Tyrrhenian Sea, near Sicily and the "toe" of Italy.) Clarke said, "Verne's imagination did not stop there; would it be possible, he asked himself, to go even further—to descend, in fact, to the very center of the Earth?" In the novel, the characters return to the surface through the crater on Stromboli.

But surely Jules Verne was inspired by more than the account of a descent a short way into the crater of a volcano. He could hardly have been unaware of the hollow-earth theories of John Cleves Symmes, one of the all-time great American crackpots.

It's true that back in 1830, when Symmes conceived his hollow-earth theory, we knew a great deal less about the interior of our planet than we do today. Still, Symmes's idea that the Earth was entirely hollow, with huge holes at either end (at the poles), was wildly farfetched even in those days. Of course, Symmes didn't see it that way; he pursued proof for his theory with the fervor of a true believer, and finally just worked himself to death trying to raise money to outfit an expedition to find the polar holes.

During his lifetime, Symmes lectured widely on his

theory and picked up a number of supporters. They kept the hollow-earth theory alive long past the time when it had been proven scientifically preposterous. Indeed, it is not quite dead yet.

Perhaps one reason Symmes's theory is still around is that the hollow Earth became so popular in fiction. Jules Verne was not the only one to set stories inside the Earth; Edgar Allan Poe and Edgar Rice Burroughs (the creator of Tarzan) did, too. The hollow Earth is also featured in a great deal of fiction by less well-known authors.

Though Symmes himself did not discuss the possibility of surviving dinosaurs inside the hollow Earth, some of his modern disciples do. One of the favorite myths among modern-day hollow-Earthers concerns polar explorer Admiral Richard E. Byrd, and the story contains hints of dinosaurs.

When Byrd flew over the South Pole in 1947, Symmes's theory should have been destroyed for all time, for Byrd found no hole at the pole. But today's hollow-Earthers insist that Byrd *did* find a hole in the pole—in fact, they say, he flew a considerable way into the hollow Earth, and there he saw gigantic animals moving through a lush, junglelike setting. It's just that these "facts" are being "covered up" by the governments of the world.

This story is obviously a complete fabrication, but dedicated hollow-Earthers (and there are a surprising number of them) insist that it is gospel. They even

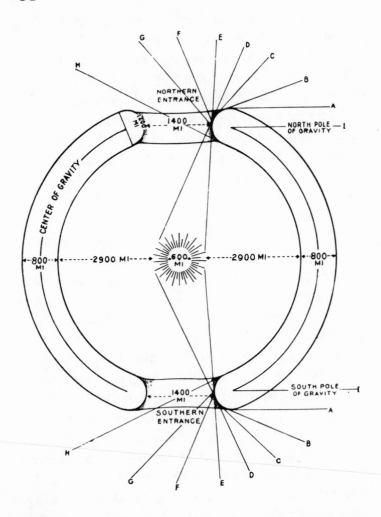

Up until the early years of the twentieth century, the idea of a hollow Earth was taken very seriously indeed by some people. Here, from a book on that subject printed in 1920, is a diagram of how the hollow Earth was supposed to look.

insist that satellite photos of the Earth taken from space are routinely doctored to hide the incredible truth—that there are holes at the poles! There is no arguing with such folk.

A Journey to the Centre of the Earth is, in my view at least, a rather dull book. And besides, dinosaurs are not central to the action. Far better, and more dinosaur oriented, too, is Arthur Conan Doyle's *The Lost World.*

Practically everyone knows that Conan Doyle created Sherlock Holmes, the world's most famous fictional character. But most people do not know that he also created another character, nearly as interesting—the bearded, barrel-chested, savage-tempered genius Professor George Edward Challenger. *The Lost World* is the first and probably the best of the Challenger novels.

In *The Lost World*, Professor Challenger leads a party of adventurers to an unexplored high plateau in South America. The place is filled with "prehistoric life." The first of the prehistoric creatures they encounter is a pterodactyl:

> The whole group of us were covered for an instant by a canopy of leathery wings, and I had a momentary vision of a long, snake-like neck, a fierce, red, greedy eye, and a great snapping beak, filled, to my amazement, with little, gleaming teeth.

Summerlee, one of the expedition members who had been openly skeptical of Challenger's lost-world theories, is very impressed by this meeting. He reaches over to take Challenger's hand and says, "I owe you an apology. Sir, I am very much in the wrong, and I beg that you will forget what is past."

There are dinosaurs aplenty. Peaceful *Iguanodons*:

> Even the babies were as big as elephants, while the two large ones were far beyond all the creatures I have ever seen. They had slate-colored skin, which was scaled like a lizard's and shimmered where the sun shone upon it. All five were sitting up, balancing themselves upon their broad, powerful tails and their huge three-toed hind feet, while with their small five-fingered front feet they pulled down the branches upon which they browsed.

And less peaceful, large carnivorous dinosaurs:

> The thing moved forward with a dreadful snarl. Lord John never hesitated, but running toward it with a quick, light step, he dashed the flaming wood into the brute's face. For one moment I had a vision of a horrible mask like a giant toad's of warty, leprous skin, and of a loose mouth all beslobbered with fresh blood.

Challenger and his intrepid band encounter and overcome a large number of other dinosaurs, too. But these are not the only "prehistoric creatures" inhabiting the South American plateau. The party also come across a particularly nasty and violent form of "ape-man." Yes, *The Lost World* did a great deal to solidify the popular idea that dinosaurs and prehistoric men were alive at the same time. Scientifically, such an idea is nonsense, and Conan Doyle, who wrote *The Lost World* in 1912, surely knew this. But it didn't matter—he was out to produce a good story, and he did. Unlike Verne's tedious *Journey*, *The Lost World* moves along at breakneck speed, and so much happens that one hardly notices, or cares, that the whole story is quite ridiculous.

A third major writer to make use of the dinosaur-encounter theme was Tarzan's creator, Edgar Rice Burroughs. Indeed, the prolific Burroughs used the theme many times. He created his own dinosaur-infested underground world—it was called Pellucidar —and set a series of short novels in it. In the novel *Tarzan at the Earth's Core*, Burroughs had Tarzan journey to the center of the Earth and meet, among other things, a flying stegosaur!

The first of the Pellucidar books was *At the Earth's Core*. Early in the novel, the hero, David Innis (who has a splendid name for an explorer of the inner Earth), passes a salt sea filled with plesiosaurs and ïchthyosaurs—they were still the best known of the ancient marine giants. Innis muses:

I had forgotten what little geology I had studied at
school—about all that remained was the impression of
horror that the illustrations of restored prehistoric
monsters had made upon me, and a well-defined belief
that any man with a pig's shank and a vivid imagination could "restore" most any sort of paleolithic monster he saw fit and take rank as a first-class
paleontologist. But when I saw these sleek shiny carcasses shimmering in the sunlight as they emerged
from the ocean, shaking their giant heads; when I saw
the waters roll from their sinuous bodies in miniature
waterfalls, as they glided hither and thither, now upon
the surface, now half submerged; as I saw them meet,
open-mouthed, hissing and snorting, in their titanic
and interminable warring, I realized how futile is
man's poor weak imagination by comparison with Nature's incredible genius.

Unquestionably Burroughs' best novels about dinosaurs are *The Land That Time Forgot* and its two
sequels, *The People That Time Forgot* and *Out of
Time's Abyss.*

The novels concern a "lost island" called Caspak.
Here, dinosaurs may be the least exotic inhabitants.
Still, they're pretty exotic:

> The creature appeared to be a great lizard at least
> ten feet high, with a huge, powerful tail as long as its
> torso, mighty hind legs, and short forelegs. When it
> had advanced from the wood, it hopped much after the
> fashion of a kangaroo, using its hind feet and tail to

propel it, and when it stood erect, it sat upon its tail. Its head was long and thick, with a blunt muzzle, and the opening of the jaws ran back to a point behind the eyes . . . the jaws were armed with long, sharp teeth. The scaly body was covered with black and yellow spots about a foot in diameter and irregular in contour. These spots were outlined in red with edgings about an inch wide. The underside of the chest, body, and tail were a greenish white.

This is one of literature's more colorful dinosaurs!

The novels of Verne, Conan Doyle, and Burroughs are the best-known fictional treatments of the dinosaur. All the books I've discussed have been reprinted many times, and all have been made into movies at least once. But fame is not necessarily an indicator of superior quality. Dinosaurs have also appeared in a number of little-known short stories. Some of these are as good as, or better than, anything written by the "big three."

In the late nineteenth and early twentieth centuries, most stories about dinosaurs concerned the possibility of encountering survivors in out-of-the-way places. Typical of this genre is "The Lizard," by Cutcliffe Hyne. This story was first published in 1898. It concerns a young man who goes exploring in a cave and comes upon some sort of prehistoric lizard preserved in limestone. As the explorer begins to knock the beast free of its limestone casing, he discovers, to his horror, that the thing isn't dead. It was just sleeping, and now it is awake—and apparently hungry:

> . . . Stirring—and alive. It was writhing and strain
> ing to leave the rocky bed where it had lain quiet
> through all those countless cycles of time, and I
> watched in a very petrifaction of terror. Its efforts
> threw up whole basketfuls of splintered stone at a
> time. I could see the muscles of its back ripple at each
> effort. I could see the exposed part of its body grow
> in size every time it wrenched at the walls of that
> semi-eternal prison.

It was, without question, a strange-looking beast:

> Its body was about the bigness of horses. Its head
> was curiously short, but the mouth opened back al
> most to the forearm; and sprouting from the nose
> were two enormous feelers, each at least six feet
> long, tipped with fleshy tendrils like fingers which
> opened and closed tremulously. In color it was a
> bright grass-green. And worst of all was the musky
> smell.

Somehow, through the energetic use of a penknife,
our hero manages to fight the monster off and escape
from the cave. But he remarks, "I go no more cave
hunting, and I offer no help to those who do."

Science fiction was more popular in the late nineteenth century than most people imagine, and the
man-meets-dinosaur theme had its limitations even
for the most convinced dinosaurophile. Some varia

tions had to be introduced just to keep the theme viable. One of the most imaginative, even bizarre treatments of the man-meets-prehistoric-monster theme was "The Monster of Lake LaMetrie." This story was written in 1899 by Wardon Allan Curtis, an early science-fiction writer who is virtually unknown today.

The story is told in the form of extracts from the diary of a doctor named James McLennegan. He explains how he has decided to go to investigate a lake in the mountains of Wyoming that is said to be inhabited by strange and very primitive fish and other creatures found nowhere else on Earth.

All of this is described in the account written by Father LaMetrie years ago, and he there advances the theory that the Earth is hollow, and that its interior is inhabited by the forms of plant and animal life which disappeared from its surface ages ago, and that the lake connects with this interior region. Symmes's theory of polar orifices is well known to you. It is amply corroborated. . . . Through the great holes at the poles the sun sends light and heat into the interior.

As you can see, Curtis assumed that Symmes's polar-hole theory was still widely known when he wrote this tale.

As his only companion on his difficult journey, Dr. McLennegan takes a young man named Edward Framingham, who decides that the trip just might improve his health. He is said to be suffering from "an acute form of dyspepsia that at times nearly [drives] him frantic." He gets a lot of pains in his stomach.

A few days after their arrival, some sort of tremendous convulsion takes place in the lake, and there appears in the water a huge *Elasmosaurus*—it seems to have been thrown up from the depths. Almost by accident the doctor slices off the top of the creature's head with a machete. Then, fearing that the thing might somehow recover and get away or attack him, the doctor removes its brain. He describes the creature thus:

> In length of body, it is exactly twenty-eight feet. In the widest part it is eight feet through laterally, and it is some six feet through from back to belly. Four great flippers, rudimentary arms and feet, and an immensely long, sinuous, swanlike neck complete the creature's body. Its head is very small for the size of the body and is very round, and a pair of long jaws project in front much like a duck's bill. Its skin is a leathery integument of lustrous black, and its eyes are enormous hazel optics with a soft, melancholy stare in their liquid depths. It is an *Elasmosaurus*, one of the largest of antediluvian animals.

Strangely enough, though the creature has had the top of its head sliced off and its brain removed, it refuses to die. The doctor marvels at its power to sustain life.

Meanwhile, poor Framingham, whose stomach pains have been getting worse and worse, thinks that he is dying. He is in such agony that he cuts his own throat. Then Dr. McLennegan gets a bright idea. He has noticed that the interior of the *Elasmosaurus*'s skull is very similar in shape to the interior of a human's skull. "It is, as nearly as I can judge, the size and shape of the brainpan of an ordinary man who wears a seven-and-an-eighth hat." So the doctor decides to try to transplant the unfortunate Framingham's brain into the empty skull of the *Elasmosaurus*. "For years the medical fraternity has been predicting that brain grafting will sometime be successfully accomplished."

And lo and behold, it *is* accomplished—the first and only successful transplant of a human brain into the body of a prehistoric monster! The *Elasmosaurus* begins to recover, and the doctor is able to communicate in a rough sort of way with Framingham's brain in the monster's body. As time passes, the human brain's control over the *Elasmosaurus* grows, until the creature not only speaks, but sings, "chanting the solemn notes of the Gregorian, the full-throated Latin words mingling with the roaring of the wind . . ." An *Elasmosaurus* that chants in medieval Latin must surely be one of the oddest and most original creations in all of science fiction!

But, as in most traditional monster tales from Mary Shelley's *Frankenstein* onward, the experiment eventually goes wrong. Ultimately the monster body begins to dominate the human brain. The doctor complains, "No longer is his conversation such as an educated man can enjoy, but slangy and diffuse iterations concerning the trivial happenings of our uneventful life. Where will it end?" The monster, it seems, has become a bore.

What follows is considerably worse than a decline in the creature's level of conversation. The tale ends with the *Elasmosaurus* tearing Dr. McLennegan to bits.

Inevitably, as the possibility of lost lands or a hollow Earth became more and more remote, the man-meets-dinosaur type of story began to fade. Finally it got to the point where dinosaurs rarely appeared in straight science fiction at all. However, very dinosaur-like dragons became a staple feature in the field of heroic fantasy. In this form of fiction, it is possible to remove dinosaurs from the Earth and put them on some distant planet or into an entirely mythic land. There is no need to keep up even the pretense of reality. Writers like Robert E. Howard often had their naked-to-the-waist "barbarian" heroes rescuing scantily clad maidens from the clutches of things that looked like dinosaurs. And Lin Carter, creator of Thongor the barbarian, has his sword-wielding hero run into such creatures regularly:

But what was that? Another roaring cry cut through the darkness! Almost upon the slowly moving boat, the larth paused, swinging its great blunt-snouted head from side to side . . . and there, breaking the black waves a few hundred feet away, was another sea monster! Another great larth, here to contend with the crippled monarch for the prize. Thongor drew in his breath. Not just one—but *two* sea dragons thirsted for their blood.

The two dragons came together with a meaty thud, clawing at each other's bellies with hooked paws, tails slashing the water into a white chaos of foam.

And so the two dinosaurian monsters battle to the death in Lin Carter's mythical world, just as, a century earlier, they had battled inside Jules Verne's hollow Earth, and in Thomas Hawkins's book about "sea dragons."

There is one way for a dinosaur-loving science-fiction writer to get around the overused lost-lands plot. If you can't bring dinosaurs into the modern world, then you can send modern man back into the dinosaurs' world through the use of time travel. Perhaps the best use of dinosaurs in a time-travel story is in L. Sprague de Camp's 1956 novelette "A Gun for a Dinosaur." This story is really one of the best in the long literary history of the dinosaur.

What makes the story so good is that de Camp is

not only a masterful writer of science fiction and fantasy, he is also a dinosaur enthusiast and quite an expert on dinosaurs. In fact, he and his wife wrote a large and excellent nonfiction book on the subject. His thorough knowledge of dinosaurs is what makes this little tale a classic.

In the story, a certain Professor Prochaska has invented a practical time machine with only one major drawback—it is enormously expensive to operate. In order to break even, he rents the machine out to wealthy sportsmen who want to go into the distant past and hunt dinosaurs. These fellows covet large and spectacular heads to hang in their dens:

> One furnishing he demanded was a ceratopsian head over the fireplace. Those are the ones with the big horned heads with the parrot-beak and a frill over the neck, you know. You have to think twice about collecting them, because if you put a seven-foot *Triceratops* head into a small living room, there's apt to be no room left for anything else.

The narrator, a professional hunter, decides (much against his better judgment) to take a couple of hunters of questionable ability back into the late Cretaceous, a time when there were really big dinosaurs.

One of the hunters is trigger-happy. He wants to shoot at everything, including a giant sauropod wallowing in a swamp. The narrator explains why this is not a good idea:

There's no point in it, and it's not sporting. First, they're almost invulnerable. They're even harder to hit in the brain than other dinosaurs because of the way they sway their heads about on those long necks. Their hearts are too deeply buried to reach unless you're awfully lucky. Then, if you kill one in the water, he sinks and can't be recovered. If you kill one on land, the only trophy is that little head. You can't bring the whole beast back because he weighs thirty tons or more, and we've got no use for thirty tons of meat.

The human hunters find that there are also hunters among the dinosaurs.

Then there was a great swishing of foliage and a wild yell from James. Something heaved up out of the shrubbery, and I saw the head of the biggest of the local flesh-eaters, *Tyrannosaurus trionyches* himself.

The scientists can insist that *rex* is the bigger species, but I'll swear this blighter was bigger than any *rex* ever hatched. It must have stood twenty feet high and been fifty feet long. I could see its big bright eye and six-inch teeth and the big dewlap that hangs down from its chin to its chest.

Since this marvelous tale has often been reprinted and thus is readily available, I won't spoil it for you by telling you what happens. Read it for yourself. And when you do, I think you will agree that dinosaur hunting is not a sport for everyone.

One of the first times dinosaurs lumbered onto the silver screen was in a very short 1917 film entitled *The Dinosaur and the Missing Link*. Naturally, they weren't real dinosaurs—they were rubber-and-metal models created by a young Californian named Willis O'Brien, who was fascinated by both animation and dinosaurs, and who was to pursue his twin interests throughout a long Hollywood career. O'Brien had once served as a guide in an area where many dinosaur fossils were found. But film was his first love.

The film technique O'Brien used in *The Dinosaur and the Missing Link* is known as stop-motion photography, and it sounds simple. You make a movable model, pose it, and then shoot one frame of film. You move the model slightly and shoot another frame. You move it just a little bit more, shoot a third frame —and so on. Eventually, when the frames are run at normal motion-picture speed, the illusion of continuous motion is created. As I said, the technique sounds simple, but in reality it takes a great deal of skill, time, and money.

Back in 1917, stop-motion photography was brand-new, and O'Brien had to feel his way, inventing and innovating at every step. He had started out with clay models, but soon discovered that they melted under movie lights. So he had to create the rubber-and-metal models. There was no real movie industry, either. O'Brien got five thousand dollars to make the film

Scene from the 1925 film version of *The Lost World.* At the time these dinosaur models were considered the height of realism.

from an entrepreneur who thought that the "puppet process" had some commercial possibilities.

O'Brien or "O'Bie," as he came to be called made a number of other short films that featured his dinosaur models. Then he did the special effects for the 1925 silent-movie version of Conan Doyle's *The Lost World.* The film starred the well-known character actor Wallace Beery as the terrible-tempered Professor Challenger, and there were a number of other well-known actors in the cast, but the real stars were O'Bie's dinosaur models.

Sir Arthur Conan Doyle himself showed some advance clips of the *Lost World* dinosaurs to a meeting of the Society of American Magicians. Conan Doyle did not explain how the films had been made, and that led some in the press to suggest that Conan Doyle really had discovered a lost world. When the film was released, it was well received by both critics and the public, and it made a great deal of money.

Undoubtedly O'Bie's greatest success came when he made the models for the original 1933 version of *King Kong.* While King Kong himself is supposed to be "prehistoric" (a term that filmmakers and authors define rather broadly), he is certainly not a dinosaur. But dinosaurs do have some memorable scenes in this film classic. In the movie, men are chased by a *Stegosaurus,* and several are killed by a *Brontosaurus.* King Kong himself battles a *Tyrannosaurus,* a plesiosaur, and a *Pteranodon.* (The *Pteranodon* has tried to carry off heroine Fay Wray, presumably as food for its young.)

In 1960, O'Brien was hired to oversee the special effects on a remake of *The Lost World.* It was to be the last film he ever did, and it would be a major disappointment, for the dinosaurs were not to be the carefully constructed models used in the original, but small lizards with plastic frills glued onto them to make them look more fearsome. The lizards would be made to look gigantic through the use of trick photography. O'Brien objected that lizards with plastic frills on them do not look like dinosaurs. But no one listened, the lizards were cheaper, and this remake of *The Lost World* is one of the most forgettable dinosaur films ever produced.

While Willis O'Brien can rightly be considered the godfather of Hollywood dinosaurs, he was certainly not the only individual responsible for getting dinosaurs onto the screen. Another important special-effects man was Ray Harryhausen, who began his career working with O'Brien.

Harryhausen's first major independent work was on a film called *The Beast from Twenty Thousand Fathoms*. This movie turned out to be a surprise smash hit, and it introduced some ideas into dinosaur films—indeed, into all monster films—that were to dominate those films for nearly a decade.

In the film, the dinosaur is called a rhedosaur (that's a made-up name), and it is inadvertently melted out of the ice at the North Pole by atomic bomb tests. *The Beast from Twenty Thousand Fathoms* came out in the 1950s. Atomic testing was going on full speed around the world, and people were worried about it—no one knew what the result might be. The monster released (or created) by atomic tests was to become a standard for monster films of the 1950s.

A giant octopus, hordes of giant ants, and even giant praying mantises came to us courtesy of atomic testing. But the rhedosaur was the first. The model used for this creature made it look exceptionally lizardlike.

The creature swims south and unaccountably decides to come ashore in New York City. The final scene of the movie takes place in the old Coney Island amusement park, where the monster dinosaur is done to death amid the tracks of the roller coaster.

By the 1950s, dinosaurs had frequently starred in films or had had major supporting roles. And they were suffering a fate many human actors have complained of—they were being typecast, either as plodding dumbbells or as ravening monsters, usually the latter.

Take for example the *Rite of Spring* segment of Walt Disney's *Fantasia*. In the opinion of many film critics, *Fantasia* was Walt Disney's most innovative movie. It consists of several pieces of classical music dramatized or illustrated by animated scenes. These range from the lyrical and humorous to the terrifying. Igor Stravinsky's *Rite of Spring* was dramatized with scenes of the "prehistoric world" in which dinosaurs were always either locked in bloody combat or facing some other form of horrible death. I was quite young when I first saw the film, and I found the dinosaurs far, far more frightening than the demons, ghosts, and goblins in the *Night on Bald Mountain* segment.

Does that mean that dinosaurs are trapped forever in the role of film heavy? Not necessarily, for movie-makers have produced at least one authentic dinosaurian hero—Godzilla. Now, I hesitate to call Godzilla a dinosaur, but I don't know what else to call him. He looks more like a fat *Tyrannosaurus* than anything else, and obviously his creators were inspired by the dinosaurs. Sure, Godzilla lives in the sea and has "atomic breath," neither of which are notable dinosaurian characteristics. And sometimes Godzilla seems to be about eighty feet tall—quite a bit taller than the largest dinosaurs. But one must allow some artistic license to Hollywood—except that Godzilla isn't from Hollywood, he is a Tokyo creation.

Japanese moviegoers love monsters, and Japanese filmmakers produce monster films by the gross. The first Japanese monster movie to make it big in the United States was *Godzilla*, released here in 1956. The picture was made on the cheap, so the special effects are not very special. Godzilla himself is played by a man in a rubber lizard suit, and looks it. Yet the movie caught on in the most astounding way, and made pots of money.

In his first movie, Godzilla does all the things a good film monster is supposed to do. He crushes cars and buildings, eats people, and generally makes a nuisance of himself. At the end of the film, he is utterly destroyed—all that is left are bones. But of course any creature as popular as Godzilla turned out to be could not be allowed to rest in peace. He has been back for at least half a dozen sequels.

Godzilla has gradually evolved from a city-stomping villain into a friendly monster, even a hero. In his later films he protects mankind against truly evil monsters like the Smog Monster, which menaces society in *Godzilla vs. the Smog Monster* (1972).

So far, dinosaurs have not fared well on television. For the most part they have been limited to the Saturday-morning cartoons—you've probably seen the phenomenally successful *Flintstones*. True, prehistoric creatures have occasionally appeared as monsters on scare series like *The Outer Limits*, which can still be seen in reruns. (In the *Outer Limits* episode called "Tourist Attraction," for example, a wealthy man goes fishing for an *Ichthyosaurus*, and, much to his horror, finds one.) And the old dinosaur movies may be shown on TV from time to time. But, mostly, television stays away from dinosaurs. Probably the reason is that dinosaurs are difficult and expensive to produce, particularly if they are to look at all real.

CHAPTER 7

Dinosaurs and Dragons

One of the richest and most important sources of dinosaur fossils in Mongolia was a place that has come to be called "The Dragon's Tomb." The name, says paleontologist Edwin Colbert, is "most appropriate."

Dinosaurs and dragons are quite similar in certain important respects. Both are generally thought of as large, powerful, and somewhat mysterious. Both are associated with ages past. The dinosaurs were the greatest and most terrible animals—monsters, if you wish—ever to walk the face of the Earth. The dragon is the greatest monster to inhabit the world of myth and legend. At times, the words "dragon" and "dinosaur" have been used interchangeably.

Many people have toyed with the idea that dragons and dinosaurs enjoy more than a poetic relationship.

Down through history, plenty of people have believed that the dragon is more than a myth. In their *Book of the Dragon*, Judy Allen and Jeanne Griffiths comment:

> Writers who give the dragon a place in zoology fall into two groups. There are those who believe that [the dragon] is a distinct species, rarely seen only because it lives in inaccessible areas of the world and is dying out. Into this group come those whose work influenced the early cartographers. And there are those who explain [the dragon] away in terms of known creatures, extant or extinct. Into this second group come most of the modern writers who have touched on the subject.

We have already examined a bit of the history of the dinosaurs; in earlier chapters I've shown how our perceptions of these creatures have changed. In order to explore the possible relationship between dinosaur and dragon, we must briefly look at the history of the dragon.

Dragon lore is extensive and complicated. What we now call the dragon has been used as a symbol by cultures throughout the world since the first known civilization. The word "dragon" itself comes from Greek, and before Greek times no special name for this kind of monster existed. What did exist were a great number of Egyptian and Mesopotamian tales of scaly monsters; in later ages, these monsters were given the title dragon.

Now, when the Greeks talked about dragons, they had something specific in mind. To the Greeks, the dragon was a big snake. The Greek word dragon meant "serpent," and was related to words meaning "sharp-eyed," which is not a bad description of a beady-eyed snake.

The Romans picked up the Greek word, and when Pliny, the influential Roman writer on natural history, described the "dragon" of India, he was quite obviously describing a large snake, probably a python. Pliny observed that this "dragon" was of such enormous size that it could "easily envelop the elephant with its folds and encircle them with its coils. The contest is equally fatal to both; the elephant, vanquished, falls to the earth and by its weight crushes the dragon which is entwined about it." Pliny had never been to India, and probably never saw a python or any other large snake. He wrote up his description after listening to travelers' tales that, while exaggerated in the extreme, were not entirely without foundation. The python *is* enormous, and it does kill its victims by wrapping itself around them and squeezing them to death. But a python could not kill an elephant, even a very small one, and would not try.

In the Bible, the words "dragon" and "serpent" are used interchangeably, and both are used as synonyms for the Devil and as symbols of evil. The ancient Hebrews, like most other peoples of the ancient Middle East, hated and feared snakes.

A twelfth-century work on natural history had this to report about the dragon: "Draco the Dragon is the biggest of all serpents, in fact, of all living things on Earth. The Greeks call it 'draconta' and [it] has been turned into Latin under the name 'draco.'"

Most of the early medieval representations of the dragon show a large legless reptile—a giant snake. These dragons sometimes had crests or crowns or even wings, but they were still basically, and quite obviously, snakes. Then, somewhere around the fifteenth century, European pictures and descriptions of dragons began to change—dragons with legs appeared on the scene. Often these dragons had only two legs, the front ones, and usually they still possessed long, snakelike bodies. But, gradually, the dragon began to look more lizardlike and less snakelike. By the seventeenth century, many people believed in the existence of a dragon that was *not* just another big snake. The learned Jesuit Father Athanasius Kircher wrote extensively on the subject of dragons. His theory was that they lived in deep subterranean caves and ventured to the surface only rarely—that was why so few people had actually seen a living dragon.

It is not surprising that when people first began to find and recognize the fossils of dinosaurs, dragons

Two versions of the medieval dragon, legless and two-legged.

came to mind. In their book on dinosaurs, L. Sprague and Catherine de Camp say:

> Soon, popular books about the fossil organisms appeared, such as *The Book of the Great Sea Dragons* (1840) by the geologist-poet Thomas Hawkins. These books were illustrated with engravings of Mesozoic

scenes showing reptiles of land, sea, and air, drawn with splendid inaccuracy . . . [the animals were] engaged in frightful battles under gloomy Gothic skies. These pictures look so much like those from medieval dragon lore that one half expects an armored knight to clatter into the scene on his destrier.

It has been suggested that the occasional discovery of dinosaur bones in medieval times (or earlier) led to many of the legends concerning the dragon. If this did happen, the dinosaurs are, in a way, directly related to dragons.

In centuries past, people in Europe and Asia often reported the discovery of "dragon bones." In China, where dragons are considered symbols of good luck, these "dragon bones" were highly valued as medicine. They were ground up and drunk in solution to cure anything from a headache to the plague. In Christian countries, "dragon bones" might be put on display in the local church as relics of the monster overcome by some local saint or hero.

Many of these "dragon bones" from East and West have been examined, and almost all of them have turned out to be the bones of long-extinct animals. But most are the bones of giant mammals—the mastodon, the woolly rhinoceros, the cave bear, and the like. These are animals that died out ten or twenty thousand years ago. The "dragon bones" are *not* the bones of dinosaurs, creatures that have been gone for over sixty million years. The bones of extinct mammals have always been far more abundant and much easier to recover than dinosaur fossils.

Now, it's not impossible that a few dinosaur fossils did get lumped in with other "dragon bones." And fossil finds sometimes did contribute directly to dragon legends. But the fossils in question always seem

The traditional Western dragon and his traditional enemy, the knight in armor.

to have been those of extinct mammals, *not* those of dinosaurs.

During the seventeenth century, several learned papers, with illustrations, were published on the subject of the many "dragon skulls" that had been found in Central Europe. What the illustrations show modern scientists is that these "dragon skulls" were, in reality, the skulls of cave bears and other extinct mammals.

The science writer Willy Ley, who had done a great deal of research into dragon lore, cited another case in which a dragon legend was based on the bones of an extinct mammal. In the marketplace in the city of Klagenfurt, Austria, Ley, wrote, there is an old and impressive monument.

The monument, fashioned about the year 1590, shows a naked giant in the act of slaying a dragon with a big spiked club. The dragon has a body similar to that of a crocodile, with bat wings attached, and [it] is furiously spitting at the giant—[it spits] fire in the legend, water in the monument. It is the skull of this dragon that is interesting. Aside from its somewhat incongruous leaf ears, it displays very clearly the outlines of the skull of woolly *Rhinoceros antiquitatis*, one of the contemporaries of the woolly mammoth. Chroniclers state that the skull of the "dragon" was found near Klagenfurt about the middle of the sixteenth century, three decades before the monument was erected. The skull itself was kept in the Town

Hall. It has been repeatedly examined by modern scientists and found to be the skull of the woolly rhinoceros.

It's possible that dinosaur fossils may, from time to time, have contributed to the growth of dragon legends. But we have no evidence that this is so, and we certainly know that dinosaur fossils could not have influenced the legends greatly. As I pointed out in Chapter 2, dinosaur fossils of any kind are rather rare in Europe. People just would not have stumbled across them very often.

A variety of "preserved dragons" were displayed throughout Europe from the fifteenth through the eighteenth centuries. Some of these became quite celebrated and were sold to collectors of "natural history" specimens for very high prices. But, without exception, these were fakes—one "dragon," for example, was a lizard with the wings of a bat sewn to it. (Taxidermists could become quite adept at creating such monstrosities.) In a time when many people were illiterate and never traveled far from home, and there were no photographs, fakes of this sort could be passed off as genuine rather easily. Needless to say, these "dragons" have nothing to do with dinosaurs.

Lacking any hard evidence to connect dinosaurs and dragons, some people have speculated that dragon legends have grown out of a "racial memory" of dinosaurs. The idea here is that we somehow carry in our minds images of the dinosaurs from the days when our ancestors confronted real dinosaurs. Supposedly these dim, subconscious "memories" of the real dinosaurs have led us to imagine a similar, yet mythical, creature—the dragon.

Even the well-known astronomer and popularizer of science Dr. Carl Sagan has speculated along these lines. In *The Dragons of Eden* he wrote:

> The most recent dinosaur fossil is dated at about sixty million years ago. The family of man (but not the genus *Homo*) is some tens of millions of years old. Could there have been manlike creatures who actually encountered *Tyrannosaurus rex?* Could there have been dinosaurs that escaped the extinctions in the late Cretaceous period? Could the pervasive dreams and common fears of "monsters," which children develop shortly after they are able to talk, be evolutionary vestiges of responses to dragons?

The boldness of such speculation is awesome. Unfortunately, there is not a shred of evidence to support theories involving "racial memory." Indeed, the weight of evidence is strongly against such theories. The only ancestors of man that were alive in the age of the dinosaurs were small insect-eating creatures somewhat like the tree shrews of today. It seems most unlikely that they would have passed along "memories" of the dinosaurs. The earliest "true man," *Homo erectus*, evolved approximately one million years ago. As I have said several times, all the evidence indicates that the dinosaurs died out sixty-five million years ago. Thus, even our most primitive ancestors would never have seen the dinosaurs, and could not have passed on "memories" of them.

Why, then, do people persist in associating dinosaurs with dragons? A great mystery? Frankly, I think not. It only seems to be a mystery because we have been asking the wrong questions and looking at the problem backwards.

The first question we must ask is not *why* the dragon resembles a dinosaur, but—does it? And the answer is, it doesn't. For the greater part of its history, the dragon was a big snake. For obscure reasons, after about the fifteenth century the snake-dragon was given legs—sometimes two, sometimes four. Its head became more prominent, and was often adorned with a crest or big ears. Occasionally the dragon had wings. But it always retained its basic snakelike appearance. It was extremely long, and even when it was given legs it looked more like a snake with legs than a proper lizard.

When Europeans encountered a somewhat similar-looking creature in Oriental mythology, they immediately assumed that it shared a common ancestry with the European dragon. But, actually, the Oriental dragon is quite different in attributes and appearance from most European dragons. And its origin is almost certainly different. The Oriental dragon has no snakes in its family tree, and if it ever was inspired by a living creature, that creature was probably the Chinese crocodile.

The Oriental dragon generally has a much larger and more elaborate head than the Western dragon. It is usually associated in one way or another with water, a trait not notable among Western dragons. And the Oriental dragon is a symbol of good luck, not a symbol of evil. So the similarities between the two kinds of dragon are only superficial. However, dragons of all types do have one thing in common: They are basically reptilian in appearance, and they are supposedly very large and powerful.

As we've seen, the dinosaurs have been classified as reptiles right from the very start. And from the very start, it was obvious that dinosaurs were very large and powerful. In these basic ways, then, dinosaurs "resembled" dragons. Many of the early reconstructions of dinosaurs and other Mesozoic giants were influenced by dragon tales. It seems unlikely that knowledge of dinosaurs bred dragon legends; rather, our "knowledge" of dragons seems to have affected our view of the dinosaurs.

Today, we have a much better idea of what dinosaurs looked like than people had a century ago. So, think about it. Does *Tyrannosaurus rex* really look like any dragon you have ever seen drawn anywhere? Certainly it doesn't. Both *Tyrannosaurus* and the

The Oriental dragon looks something like the Western dragon, but has a very different origin.

dragon have big toothy heads. But the most obvious feature of *Tyrannosaurus* (indeed, of most dinosaurs) is that it is bipedal—it walks around on its large, powerful hind legs. Dragons just aren't built that way—they look like either snakes or very long lizards. The earlier (and thus more authentic) the drawing of the dragon, the more snakelike and the less dinosaurlike it looks. Even when a dragon is shown with two legs, these are almost always the front legs, which were tiny in most dinosaurs.

I think it is safe to say that the only real connection between dinosaurs and dragons is an emotional connection that has grown up in the century and a half since dinosaurs were discovered. I also think most people would agree that while dragons may be interesting, dinosaurs are a lot more interesting. Dragons are only legendary monsters. But when you go to a natural history museum, you can see the bones of the most fabulous real-life monsters ever to roam our planet . . . the dinosaurs.

For Further Reading

NONFICTION

Adler, Alan, ed. *Science Fiction and Horror Movie Posters*. New York: Dover Publications, 1977.

Allen, Judy, and Griffiths, Jeanne. *The Book of the Dragon*. Secaucus, N.J.: Chartwell Books, 1979.

Cohen, Daniel. *A Modern Look at Monsters*. New York: Dodd, Mead & Co., 1970.

————. *What Really Happened to the Dinosaurs?* New York: E. P. Dutton & Co., 1977.

Colbert, Edwin H. *Dinosaurs: Their Discovery and Their World*. New York: E. P. Dutton & Co., 1961.

————. *Men and Dinosaurs*. New York: E. P. Dutton & Co., 1968.

de Camp, L. Sprague, and de Camp, Catherine C. *The*

Day of the Dinosaur. Garden City, N.Y.: Double-day & Co., 1968.

Desmond, Adrian J. *The Hot-Blooded Dinosaurs.* New York: Dial Press, 1976.

Gerani, Gary, and Schulman, Paul. *Fantastic Television.* New York: Harmony Books, 1977.

Heuvelmans, Bernard. *In the Wake of the Sea Serpents.* New York: Hill & Wang, 1968.

————. *On the Track of Unknown Animals.* New York: Hill & Wang, 1959.

Ingersoll, Ernest. *Dragons and Dragon Lore.* New York: Payson and Clarke, 1928.

Ley, Willy. *Dragons in Amber.* New York: Viking Press, 1951.

————. *The Lungfish and the Unicorn.* New York: Modern Age, 1941.

Romer, Alfred S. *Vertebrate Paleontology.* Chicago: University of Chicago Press, 1945.

Rovin, Jeff. *From the Land Beyond: The Films of Willis O'Brien and Ray Harryhausen.* Berkley Publishing, 1977.

Sagan, Carl. *The Dragons of Eden.* New York: Random House, 1977.

Seeley, Harry G. *Dragons of the Air.* New York: Dover Publications, 1967.

Wendt, Herbert. *Before the Deluge.* Garden City, N.Y.: Doubleday & Co., 1968.

White, T. H. *The Bestiary: A Book of Beasts.* New York: G. P. Putnam's Sons, 1954.

FICTION

Burroughs, Edgar Rice. *At the Earth's Core.* Garden City, N.Y.: Nelson Doubleday, n.d.

———. *The Land That Time Forgot.* Garden City, N.Y.: Nelson Doubleday, n.d.

Carter, Lin. *Thongor and the Dragon City.* New York: Berkley Publishing, 1970.

de Camp, L. Sprague. *The Best of L. Sprague de Camp.* Garden City, N.Y.: Nelson Doubleday, 1978.

Doyle, Arthur Conan. *The Lost World.* New York: Looking Glass Library, 1959.

Evans, Hilary, and Evans, Dik. *Beyond the Gaslight: Science in Popular Fiction, 1885–1905.* New York: Vanguard Press, 1977.

Haining Peter, ed. *The Ancient Mysteries Reader.* Garden City, N.Y.: Doubleday & Co., 1975.

Verne, Jules, *A Journey to the Centre of the Earth.* New York: Dodd, Mead & Co., 1959.

Index